Books by Yukio Mishima

After the Banquet

Confessions of a Mask

Five Modern Nō Plays

Forbidden Colors

Madame de Sade

Runaway Horses

The Sailor Who Fell from Grace with the Sea

Spring Snow

The Sound of Waves

The Temple of the Golden Pavilion

Thirst for Love

The Sailor Who Fell from Grace

with the Sea

The Sailor Who Fell

TRANSLATED FROM THE JAPANESE
BY JOHN NATHAN

from Grace with the Sea

by YUKIO MISHIMA

CHARLES E. TUTTLE COMPANY
Suido 1-chome, 2-6, Bunkyo-ku, Tokyo

Originally published in Japanese as *Gogo no Eiko*

Published by the Charles E. Tuttle Company, Inc., of Rutland, Vermont and Tokyo, Japan, with editorial offices at Suido 1-chome, 2–6, Bunkyo-ku, Tokyo, Japan, by special arrangement with Alfred A. Knopf, Inc., New York.

First Tuttle edition, 1967
Twelfth printing, 1990

Lyrics for the song which appears for the first time on pages 17–18, "I Can't Give Up the Sailor's Life," are from a poem by Ryo Yano.

PRINTED IN JAPAN

CONTENTS

CONTENTS

SUMMER

CHAPTER ONE

"Sleep well, dear."

Noboru's mother closed his bedroom door and locked it. What would she do if there were a fire? Let him out first thing—she had promised herself that. But what if the wooden door warped in the heat or paint clogged the keyhole? The window? There was a gravel path below; besides, the second floor of this gangling house was hopelessly high.

It was all his own fault. It would never have happened if he hadn't let the chief persuade him to sneak out of the house that night. There had been endless questions afterward, but he hadn't revealed the chief's name.

They lived at the top of Yado Hill in Yokohama, in a house his father had built. After the war the house had been requisitioned by the Occupation Army and toilets had been installed in each of the upstairs bedrooms:

being locked in at night was no great discomfort, but to a thirteen-year-old the humiliation was enormous.

Left alone one morning to watch the house and in need of something to vent his spite on, Noboru began to rummage through his room.

A large chest of drawers was built into the wall adjoining his mother's bedroom. He pulled out all the drawers, and as he was dumping their contents onto the floor he noticed a trickle of light spilling into one of the empty compartments of the chest.

He thrust his head into the space and discovered the source of the light: strong summer sunlight was reflecting off the sea into his mother's empty bedroom. There was plenty of room in the chest. Even a grownup might squeeze in up to his belly if he lay flat. Peering at his mother's bedroom through the peephole, Noboru sensed something new and fresh about it.

The shiny brass beds his father had ordered from New Orleans were set against the wall on the left side just as they had been before his death. A bedspread was smoothed neatly over one of them, and on the white cloth a large letter "K"—Kuroda was the family name. A blue straw sun hat, trailing a long pale-blue ribbon, lay on the bed. On the night table stood a blue electric fan.

Across the room, near the window, there was a dressing table fitted with an oval three-piece mirror. The mirror was not quite closed; the upper edges of the glass glinted through the cracks like splinters of ice. In front of the mirror rose a small city of bottles: eau de Cologne, perfume sprays, lavender toilet water, a Bohemian glass goblet, facets glittering in the light . . . a crumpled pair of brown-lace gloves lay withering like cedar leaves.

A couch and two chairs, a floor lamp, and a low, delicate table were arranged directly under the window. An embroidery frame, the beginnings of a pattern needled into the silk, was propped on the couch. The vogue for such things had passed long ago, but his mother loved all kinds of handicraft. The pattern seemed to be the wings of some gaudy bird, a parrot maybe, on a background of silver-gray. A pair of stockings lay in a heap next to the embroidery. The shocking embrace of sheer nylon and the imitation damask of the couch gave the room an air of agitation. She must have noticed a run on her way out and changed in a hurry.

Only dazzling sky and a few fragments of cloud, hard and glossy as enamel in the light bouncing off the water, could be seen through the window.

Noboru couldn't believe he was looking at his mother's bedroom; it might have belonged to a stranger. But there was no doubt that a woman lived there: femininity trembled in every corner, a faint scent lingered in the air.

Then a strange idea assailed him. Did the peephole

just happen to be here, an accident? Or—after the war —when the soldiers' families had been living together in the house. . . . He had a sudden feeling that another body, larger than his, a blond, hairy body, had once huddled in this dusty space in the wall. The thought soured the close air and he was sickened. Wriggling backwards out of the chest, he ran to the next room. He would never forget the queer sensation he had when, flinging open the door, he burst in.

Drab and familiar, the room bore no resemblance to the mysterious chamber he had seen through the peep-hole: it was here that he came to whine and to sulk— *it's time you stopped coming into Mother's room so often with that excuse about wanting to watch the ships; you're not a child any more, dear*—here that his mother would put aside her embroidery to help him with his homework while she stifled yawns, or would scold him for not tying his necktie straight, or would check the ledgers she brought home from the shop. . . .

He looked for the peephole. It wasn't easy to find. Cunningly hidden in the ornately carved wainscot, in a spot on the upper border where the rippled pattern overlapped to conceal it—a very small hole.

Noboru stumbled back to his room, gathered the scattered clothing, and stuffed it back into the drawers. When everything was as it had been, he vowed never to do anything that might attract the grownups' attention to the chest.

Shortly after he made this discovery, Noboru began spying on his mother at night, particularly when she had nagged or scolded him. The moment his door was closed he would slip the drawer quietly out of the chest, and then watch in unabating wonder while she prepared for bed. On nights when she was gentle, he never looked.

He discovered that it was her habit, though the nights were not yet uncomfortably hot, to sit completely naked for a few minutes before going to bed. He had a terrible time when she went near the wall mirror, for it hung in a corner of the room he couldn't see.

She was only thirty-three and her slender body, shapely from playing tennis every week, was beautiful. Usually she got right into bed after touching her flesh with perfumed water, but sometimes she would sit at the dressing table and gaze into the mirror at her profile for minutes at a time, eyes hollow as though ravaged by fever, scented fingers rooted between her thighs. On those nights, mistaking the crimson of her bundled nails for blood, Noboru trembled.

Never had he observed a woman's body so closely. Her shoulders, like the shoreline, sloped gently downward. Her neck and arms were lightly tanned, but at her chest, as if an inner lamp were burning, began a zone of warm, fleshy white. Her haughty breasts inclined sharply away from her body; and when she kneaded them with her hands, the rosy nipples danced apart. He saw the trembling belly. And the scar that meant she had borne children. A dusty red book in his father's study had taught him that; he had discovered it on the highest shelf, turned the wrong way, sandwiched between a gardening book and a pocket business manual.

And the zone of black. The angle was bad somehow, and he strained until the corners of his eyes began to ache. He tried all the obscenity he knew, but words alone couldn't penetrate that thicket. His friends were probably right when they called it a pitiful little vacant house. He wondered if that had anything to do with the emptiness of his own world.

At thirteen, Noboru was convinced of his own genius (each of the others in the gang felt the same way) and certain that life consisted of a few simple signals and decisions; that death took root at the moment of birth and man's only recourse thereafter was to water and tend it; that propagation was a fiction; consequently, society was a fiction too: that fathers and teachers, by virtue of being fathers and teachers, were guilty of a grievous sin. Therefore, his own father's death, when he was eight, had been a happy incident, something to be proud of.

On moonlit nights his mother would turn out the lights and stand naked in front of the mirror! Then he would lie awake for hours, fretted by visions of emptiness. An ugliness unfurled in the moonlight and soft shadow and suffused the whole world. If I were an amoeba, he thought, with an infinitesimal body, I could defeat ugliness. A man isn't tiny or giant enough to defeat anything.

As he lay in bed, ships' horns often screeched like nightmares through his open window. When his mother had been gentle, he was able to sleep without looking. On those nights, the vision appeared in his dreams instead.

He never cried, not even in his dreams, for hardheartedness was a point of pride. A large iron anchor withstanding the corrosion of the sea and scornful of the barnacles and oysters that harass the hulls of ships, sinking polished and indifferent through heaps of broken glass, toothless combs, bottle caps, and prophylactics into the mud at harbor bottom—that was how he liked to imagine his heart. Someday he would have an anchor tattooed on his chest.

The most ungentle night of all came toward the end of summer vacation. Suddenly: there was no way of knowing it would happen.

His mother left early in the evening, explaining that she had invited Second Mate Tsukazaki to dinner. To thank him, she said, for having shown Noboru around his ship the day before. She was wearing a kimono of black lace over a crimson under-robe; her obi was white brocade: Noboru thought she looked beautiful as she left the house.

At ten o'clock she returned with Tsukazaki. Noboru let them in and sat in the living room with the tipsy sailor, listening to stories about the sea. His mother interrupted at ten-thirty, saying it was time for him to go to bed. She hurried Noboru upstairs and locked the bedroom door.

The night was humid, the space inside the chest so stuffy he could scarcely breathe: he crouched just outside, ready to steal into position when the time came, and waited. It was after midnight when he heard stealthy footsteps on the stairs. Glancing up, he saw the doorknob turning eerily in the darkness as someone tried the door; that had never happened before. When he heard his mother's door open a minute later, he squeezed his sweating body into the chest.

The moonlight, shining in from the south, was reflected back from one pane of the wide-open window. Tsukazaki was leaning against the window sill; there were gold-braid epaulets on his white short-sleeved shirt. His mother's back came into view, crossed the room to the sailor: they embraced in a long kiss. Finally, touching the buttons on his shirt, she said something in a low voice, then turned on the dim floor lamp and moved out of sight. It was in front of the clothes closet, in a corner of the room he couldn't see, that she began to undress. The sharp hiss of the sash unwinding, like a serpent's warning, was followed by a softer, swishing sound as the kimono slipped to the floor. Suddenly the air around the peephole was heavy with the scent of Arpège. She had walked perspiring and a little drunk through the humid night air and her body, as she undressed, exhaled a musky fragrance which Noboru didn't recognize.

The sailor was still at the window, staring straight at Noboru. His sunburned face was featureless except for the eyes that glittered in the lamplight. By comparing him with the lamp, which he had often used as a yardstick, Noboru was able to estimate his height. He was certainly no more than five feet seven, probably a little less. Not such a big man.

Slowly, Tsukazaki unbuttoned his shirt, then slipped easily out of his clothes. Though he must have been nearly the same age as Noboru's mother, his body looked younger and more solid than any landsman's: it might have been cast in the matrix of the sea. His broad shoulders were square as the beams in a temple roof, his chest strained against a thick mat of hair, knotted muscle like twists of sisal hemp bulged all over his body: his flesh looked like a suit of armor that he could cast off at will. Then Noboru gazed in wonder as, ripping up through the thick hair below the belly, the lustrous temple tower soared triumphantly erect.

The hair on his rising and falling chest scattered

quivering shadows in the feeble light; his dangerous, glittering gaze never left the woman as she undressed. The reflection of the moonlight in the background traced a ridge of gold across his shoulders and conjured into gold the artery bulging in his neck. It was authentic gold of flesh, gold of moonlight and glistening sweat. His mother was taking a long time to undress. Maybe she was delaying purposely.

Suddenly the full long wail of a ship's horn surged through the open window and flooded the dim room—a cry of boundless, dark, demanding grief; pitch-black and glabrous as a whale's back and burdened with all the passions of the tides, the memory of voyages beyond counting, the joys, the humiliations: the sea was screaming. Full of the glitter and the frenzy of night, the horn thundered in, conveying from the distant offing, from the dead center of the sea, a thirst for the dark nectar in the little room.

Tsukazaki turned with a sharp twist of his shoulders and looked out toward the water.

It was like being part of a miracle: in that instant everything packed away inside Noboru's breast since the first day of his life was released and consummated. Until the horn sounded, it was only a tentative sketch. The finest materials had been prepared and all was in readiness, verging on the unearthly moment. But one element was lacking: the power needed to transfigure those motley sheds of reality into a gorgeous palace.

Then, at a signal from the horn, the parts merged into a perfect whole.

Assembled there were the moon and a feverish wind, the incited, naked flesh of a man and a woman, sweat, perfume, the scars of a life at sea, the dim memory of ports around the world, a cramped breathless peephole, a young boy's iron heart—but these cards from a gypsy deck were scattered, prophesying nothing. The universal order at last achieved, thanks to the sudden, screaming horn, had revealed an ineluctable circle of life—the cards had paired: Noboru and mother—mother and man—man and sea—sea and Noboru. . . .

He was choked, wet, ecstatic. Certain he had watched a tangle of thread unravel to trace a hallowed figure. And it would have to be protected: for all he knew, he was its thirteen-year-old creator.

"If this is ever destroyed, it'll mean the end of the world," Noboru murmured, barely conscious. *I guess I'd do anything to stop that, no matter how awful!*

CHAPTER TWO

Surprised, Ryuji Tsuka-
zaki woke up in an unfamiliar bed. The bed next to his
was empty. Little by little, he recalled what the woman
had told him before she had fallen asleep: Noboru was
going swimming with friends in Kamakura in the morning; she would get up early and wake him, and would
come back to the bedroom as soon as he left . . . would
he please wait for her quietly. He groped for his watch
on the night table and held it up to the light that fil-
tered through the curtains. Ten minutes to eight: probably the boy was still in the house.

He had slept for about four hours, after falling
asleep at just the time he would ordinarily be going to
bed after night watch. It had been hardly more than a
nap, yet his head was clear, the long pleasure of the
night still coiled inside him tight as a spring. He
stretched and crossed his wrists in front of him. In the

light from the window, the hair on his muscled arms appeared to eddy into golden pools; he was satisfied.

Though still early, it was very hot. The curtains hung motionless in front of the open window. Stretching again, Ryuji, with one extended finger, pushed the button on the fan.

Fifteen minutes to Second Officer's watch—stand by please. He had heard the Quartermaster's summons distinctly in a dream. Every day of his life, Ryuji stood watch from noon to four and again from midnight to four in the morning. Stars were his only companions, and the sea.

Aboard the freighter *Rakuyo*, Ryuji was considered unsociable and eccentric. He had never been good at gabbing, never enjoyed the scuttlebutt supposed to be a sailor's only source of pleasure. Tales of women, anecdotes from shore, the endless boasting . . . he hated the lowbrow chatter meant to sweeten loneliness, the ritual of affirming ties with the brotherhood of men.

Whereas most men choose to become sailors because they like the sea, Ryuji had been guided by an antipathy to land. The Occupation interdict forbidding Japanese vessels to travel the open sea had been revoked just as he was graduated from a merchant-marine high school, and he had shipped out on the first freighter since the war to sail to Taiwan and Hong Kong. Later he had been to India and eventually to Pakistan.

What a joy the tropics were! Hoping to trade for nylons or wrist watches, native children met them at every port with bananas and pineapples and papayas, bright-colored birds and baby monkeys. And Ryuji loved the groves of wine palms mirrored in a muddy, slow-flowing river. Palms must have been common to his native land in some earlier life, he thought, or they could never have bewitched him so.

But as the years passed, he grew indifferent to the lure of exotic lands. He found himself in the strange predicament all sailors share: essentially he belonged neither to the land nor to the sea. Possibly a man who hates the land should dwell on shore forever. Alienation and the long voyages at sea will compel him once again to dream of it, torment him with the absurdity of longing for something that he loathes.

Ryuji hated the immobility of the land, the eternally unchanging surfaces. But a ship was another kind of prison.

At twenty, he had been passionately certain: *there's just one thing I'm destined for and that's glory; that's right, glory!* He had no idea what kind of glory he wanted, or what kind he was suited for. He knew only that in the depths of the world's darkness was a point of light which had been provided for him alone and would draw near someday to irradiate him and no other.

And it seemed increasingly obvious that the world would have to topple if he was to attain the glory that was rightfully his. They were consubstantial: glory and the capsized world. He longed for a storm. But life aboard ship taught him only the regularity of natural law and the dynamic stability of the wobbling world. He began to examine his hopes and dreams one by one, and one by one to efface them as a sailor pencils out the days on the calendar in his cabin.

Sometimes, as he stood watch in the middle of the night, he could feel his glory knifing toward him like a shark from some great distance in the darkly heaping sea, see it almost, aglow like the noctilucae that fire the water, surging in to flood him with light and cast the silhouette of his heroic figure against the brink of man's world. On those nights, standing in the white pilot-house amid a clutter of instruments and bronze signal bells, Ryuji was more convinced than ever:

There must be a special destiny in store for me; a glittering, special-order kind no ordinary man would be permitted.

At the same time, he liked popular music. He bought all the new records and learned them by heart while at sea and hummed the tunes when he had a minute, stopping when anyone came near. He liked sailor songs (the rest of the crew scorned them) and his favorite was one called "I Can't Give Up the Sailor's Life."

The whistle wails and streamers tear,
Our ship slips away from the pier.

Now the sea's my home, I decided that.

But even I must shed a tear

    As I wave, boys, as I wave so sad

    At the harbor town where my heart was glad.

As soon as the noon watch was over he would shut himself up in his darkening cabin and play the record again and again until it was time for dinner. He always turned the volume down because he didn't want to share the song; besides, he was afraid a fellow officer might drop in with some scuttlebutt if he happened to hear the music. The rest of the crew knew how he felt and no one ever disturbed him.

Sometimes, as he listened to the song or hummed it, tears brimmed in his eyes, just as in the lyrics. Strange that a man with no ties should become sentimental about a "harbor town," but the tears welled directly from a dark, distant, enervated part of himself he had neglected all his life and couldn't command.

The actual sight of land receding into the distance never made him cry. Wharf and docks, cranes and the roofs of warehouses slipping quietly away, he watched with contempt in his eye. Once the cast-off had lighted a fire in his breast, but more than ten years at sea had quelled those flames. He had gained only his sunburn and keen eyes.

Ryuji stood watch and slept, woke up, stood watch and slept again. He was full of unexpressed feelings, and his savings steadily increased, for he tried to be

alone as much as possible. He became expert at shoot-
ing the sun, he counted the stars as friends, he mastered
the arts of mooring and warping and towing until finally, listening to the din of waves at night, his ear
could discern the surge of the sea from the slake. While
he grew more familiar with lustrous tropical clouds and
the many-colored coral seas, the total in his bankbook
climbed and now he had almost two million yen* in the
bank, an extraordinary sum for a Second Mate.

He had sampled the pleasures of dissipation too. He
had lost his virginity on his first cruise. They were in
Hong Kong, and a senior officer had taken him to a
Chinese whore. . . .

Ryuji lay on the bed letting the fan scatter his cigarette ashes and half closed his eyes as if to measure on a
balance the quantity and quality of the previous night's
pleasure against the pitiful sensations of that first expe-
rience. Staring into space, he began to see again at the
back of his mind the dark wharves of Hong Kong at
night, the turbid heaviness of water lapping at the pier,
the sampans' feeble lanterns . . .

In the distance, beyond the forest of masts and the
lowered straw-mat sails of the moored fleet, the glaring
windows and neon signs of Hong Kong outshone the
weak lanterns in the foreground and tinted the black
water with their colors. Ryuji and the older seaman

* In the neighborhood of five thousand dollars; one dollar=360 yen.
[Trans.]

who was his guide were in a sampan piloted by a middle-aged woman. The oar in the stern whispered through the water as they slipped across the narrow harbor. When they came to the place where the flickering lights were clustered, Ryuji saw the girls' rooms bobbing brightly on the water.

The fleet was moored in three long lines so as to form an inner court of water. All the sterns were faced in and were decorated with sticks of burning incense and red and green paper flags celebrating regional deities. Flowery silk cloth lined the semicircular tarpaulin shells on the flat decks. At the rear of each shell a raised stand, draped with the same material, held a small mirror: an image of Ryuji's sampan wobbled from room to room as they slipped past.

The girls pretended not to notice them. Some lay swaddled in quilts, baring to the cold only dollish, powder-white necks. Others, quilts wrapped around their thighs, played with fortunetelling cards. The luscious reds and golds on the faces of the cards glittered between slender sallow fingers.

"Which one do you want?" the officer asked. "They're all young."

Ryuji didn't answer. He was about to choose the first woman in his life and, having traveled sixteen hundred leagues to this bit of dirty, reddish seaweed afloat in the turbid waters of Hong Kong, he felt curiously fatigued, perplexed. But the girls certainly were

young, and attractive. He chose before the older man
had a chance to offer a suggestion.

The whore had been sitting in silence, her face
puckered in the cold, but as Ryuji stepped onto her
boat, she laughed happily. And he found himself halfheartedly believing in the happiness he was bringing
her. She drew the flowery curtain over the entrance to
the shell.

They performed in silence. He trembled a little out
of vanity, as when he had first scaled the mast. The
woman's lower body, like a hibernating animal half
asleep, moved lethargically under the quilts; he sensed
the stars of night tilting dangerously at the top of the
mast. The stars slanted into the south, swung to the
north, wheeled, whirled into the east, and seemed finally to be impaled on the tip of the mast. By the time
he realized this was a woman, it was done. . . .

There was a knock on the door and Fusako Kuroda
came into the room with a large breakfast tray. "I'm
sorry you had to wait so long. Noboru just left a minute
ago." Putting the tray down on the tea table, she
opened the curtains and the window. "There's not a
bit of breeze. It's going to be hot again."

Even the shade beneath the window ledge was as
hot as burning asphalt. Ryuji sat up in bed and
wrapped the wrinkled sheet around his waist. Fusako
was dressed to go out. Her bare arms, moving not to

embrace him but to pour morning coffee into cups, seemed unfamiliar. They were no longer the arms of the night.

Ryuji beckoned Fusako to the bed and kissed her. The thin, sensitive skin of her lips betrayed the fluttering of her eyes: this morning, he knew, she was uneasy even while her eyes were closed.

"What time do you go to work?" he said.

"As long as I can be there by eleven. What are you going to do?"

"I might go down to the dock for a while, just to see what's going on."

They had created in a single night a new situation and now it appeared to bewilder them. For the moment, their bewilderment was their only etiquette. Ryuji, with what he liked to call the unbelievable arrogance of intolerable people, was calculating how far he might be able to go.

The expression on Fusako's radiant face suggested a number of things. Resurrection. Or an utter effacement from memory. Or even determination to prove to herself and the world that it had not, in any sense of the word, been a *mistake*.

"Shall we eat over here?" she suggested, moving to the couch. Ryuji jumped out of bed and threw on his clothes. Fusako was standing at the window. "I wish we could see your ship from here."

"If that pier wasn't so far out of town . . ." Coming

up behind her, Ryuji put his arms around Fusako's waist. Together they looked out at the harbor.

The window overlooked the red roofs of old warehouses. A block of new warehouses, like concrete apartment buildings, hulked up from the pier to the north. The canal was buried under sculls and barges. Beyond the warehouse district piles of seasoning lumber merged into an intricate wooden mosaic. Extending like a concrete finger from the seaward side of the lumber yards, a long breakwater stretched all the way to the sea.

The summer morning sun lay as thin as a dazzling sheet of hammered metal across the colossal anvil of the harbor scene.

Ryuji's fingers touched her nipples through the blue cotton dress. She tossed her head, her hair tickled his nose. As always, he felt as if he had traveled some huge distance, sometimes from the far side of the world, finally to arrive at a point of delicate sensation—a thrilling in his fingertips near a window on a summer morning.

The fragrance of coffee and marmalade filled the room.

"There was something about Noboru this morning, almost as if he knew. Of course, he seems to like you a lot, so it doesn't matter really. . . . I still don't understand how this could have happened. I mean"—her confusion rang a little false—"it's just incredible!"

CHAPTER THREE

R EX, LTD., was one of the oldest and best-known luxury shops in Yokohama's swank Motomachi district. Since her husband's death, Fusako had been running the business by herself. The Moorish architecture of the small two-story building was distinctive; the Mosque window set into the thick white wall at the front of the shop always contained a tasteful display. Inside, an open mezzanine much like a veranda overlooked a patio of imported Spanish tile. A small fountain bubbled in the center of the patio. A bronze Bacchus, some Vivax neckties carelessly draped over its arms, was one of the many curios collected by Fusako's husband before his death; these were priced so as to discourage any would-be buyer.

Fusako employed an elderly manager and four salesgirls. Among the clientele were wealthy foreigners who lived in Yokohama, a large number of dandies and movie people from Tokyo, and even some buyers from small retail shops on the Ginza who came down to forage: Rex enjoyed a reputation for uncanny discernment of fine quality, particularly in imported men's wear and accessories. Both Fusako and the manager, a man called Shibuya, who possessed her husband's tastes, were scrupulous buyers.

Whenever a ship docked in Yokohama, an import agent who was an old friend of the family used his connections to get them into the bonded warehouse as soon as the cargo had been unloaded: often Fusako was able to place a bid before other buyers had seen the shipment. Her policy was to emphasize quality labels while providing a wide price range in every item. Rex's order for Jaeger sweaters, for example, would be divided equally between the manufacturer's most exclusive and more modest lines. The same was true of imported Italian leather: Rex's selection included leather from the tanning school attached to the Chiesa Santa Croce in Florence as well as the most expensive gloves and purses from the Via Condotti.

Though Fusako was unable to travel abroad herself, because of Noboru, she had sent Mr. Shibuya on a buying trip to Europe the year before, and he had established new connections all over the Continent. Shibuya had devoted his life to elegance in dress: Rex even stocked English spats, an article not to be found in any of the Ginza shops.

Fusako reached the shop at the usual time and was greeted with the usual morning cordiality. She asked a few business questions and then went up to her office on the mezzanine and opened the day's mail. The air conditioner in the window whirred solemnly.

Being able to sit at her desk at the usual time was a great relief. It had to be this way. Today of all days, she couldn't imagine what might have happened if she had stayed home from work.

She took a lady's cigarette from her purse and glanced, as she lit it, at the memo book on her desk. Yoriko Kasuga, a movie actress in Yokohama on location, was due to arrive at noon for some colossal shopping: she had just returned from a film festival in Europe and, having spent all her gift money on other things, hoped to cover up with presents from Rex. "Some stunning French accessories," she had telephoned to say, "for about twenty men—pick out whatever you like." Later in the afternoon, a private secretary from Yokohama Importers was coming over to pick up some of the Italian polo shirts her boss, the company president, wore on the golf links. Faithful customers, these women were remarkably easy to please.

A part of the patio was visible beneath the louvered swinging doors. It was hushed. The tips of leaves on a rubber tree in one corner shone with a dull luster. Apparently no one had arrived yet.

Fusako was worried that Mr. Shibuya might have noticed what felt to her like a flush around her eyes. The old man looked at a woman as though he were examining a piece of fabric in his hand. Even if she was his employer.

She had never actually counted until that morning: five years since her husband's death! It hadn't seemed so long in passing, but all of a sudden, like a white obi she would never be able to wind up, five years was a dizzying length.

Fusako teased the ashtray with her cigarette and then snuffed it out. The man still nested in every nook of her body. She was aware of her flesh beneath the clothes as continuous, thigh and breast in warm accordance: it was a new sensation. And she could still smell the sweat of the man. As if to test them, she curled her stockinged toes.

Fusako had met Ryuji for the first time two days before. Noboru, who was a fanatic about ships, had wheedled her into asking a shipping executive friend for a letter of introduction, and they had gone to see the *Rakuyo*, a ten-thousand-ton freighter anchored at Takashima Pier. . . .

Stopping for a minute at the far end of the dock, mother and son gazed at the cream-and-green-colored ship gleaming in the distance. Fusako unfurled a parasol with a long white snakeskin handle.

"You see those ships out in the offing?" Noboru said knowingly. "They're all waiting their turn for a berth to open up."

"That's why our shipments are always so late getting in," Fusako drawled. She felt hot just looking up at the ship.

The cloud-dappled sky was partitioned by an intricate crisscross of hawsers; and lifting up at it in reverence like a slender chin was the *Rakuyo*'s prow, limitlessly high, the green banner of the fleet fluttering at its crest. The anchor clung to the hawsehole like a large metal-black crab.

"This is going to be great," Noboru said, brimming over with boyish excitement. "I guess we'll be able to look her over fore and aft."

"Let's not expect too much, dear, until we're certain this letter is what we need."

Thinking about it later, Fusako realized that she had felt her heart begin to dance even as they had stood looking up at the ship. *That's funny: I'm just as excited as Noboru.*

The feeling beset her at the height of her languor—just lifting her head was a hot and wearisome chore—suddenly and for no reason.

"She's a flush deck, Mom—looks like a pretty good ship all right." Unable to contain the knowledge that crowded his brain, Noboru held forth to his disinterested mother; as they drew closer, the *Rakuyo* swelled before them like great music. Noboru sprinted ahead and raced up the glittering, silvery gangplank.

But Fusako had to wander down the corridor in front of the officers' quarters, helplessly clutching her letter to the Captain. The decks, where unloading was in progress, were bustling and noisy, but the stuffy corridor was unpleasantly hushed.

Then a cabin door marked "Second Officer" opened and Tsukazaki appeared.

"Can you tell me where I might find the Captain?"

"He's not here now. Can I help you?"

Fusako showed him the letter; Noboru, eyes shining, gaped up at the sailor.

"I see—a kind of study trip. I suppose I can show you around." His manner was brusque, his gaze never left her face as he spoke.

That was their first encounter. She would never forget his eyes as he confronted her in the corridor. Deep-set in the disgruntled, swarthy face, they sought her out as though she were a tiny spot on the horizon, the first sign of a distant ship. That, at least, was the feeling she had. Eyes viewing an object so near had no business piercing that way, focusing so sharply—without leagues of sea between them, it was unnatural. She wondered if all eyes that endlessly scanned the horizon were that way. Unlooked-for signs of a ship descried— misgivings and delight, wariness and expectation . . . the sighted vessel just barely able to forgive the affront because of the vast reach of sea between them: a ravaging gaze. The sailor's eyes made her shudder.

Tsukazaki took them to the bridge first. The ladder they climbed to the main deck was obliquely runged with bars of summer sunlight. Indicating the freighters anchored offshore, Noboru repeated his knowing observation: "I guess all those ships are waiting their turn for a berth—"

"Right you are, sonny. Some of them may have to wait out there four or five days."

"Do they notify you on the wireless when a berth opens?"

"Right again. You get a cable from the company. There's a committee that meets every day to decide berth priorities."

Sweat was dappling Tsukazaki's white shirt with little spots which revealed the flesh of his powerful back; Fusako was disconcerted. She was grateful to the man for taking Noboru seriously but he made her uncomfortable when he turned to her and asked direct questions: "The boy knows what he's talking about. Does he want to be a sailor?" His eyes probed her again.

He seemed a rugged, simple man, yet there was also about him an air of indifference and Fusako couldn't determine whether he felt any professional pride. When, opening her parasol against the sun and peering narrowly up at his face, she tried to decide, she thought she discovered something unexpected in the shadow of his heavy brows. Something she had never seen in the broad light of day.

"He'd be smart to forget about it if he is. This is a miserable business if ever there was one," Tsukazaki said, not bothering to wait for her answer. "Over here, sonny; this is a mounted sextant." The instrument he slapped looked like a white mushroom on a long stem.

When they went into the pilothouse, Noboru wanted to touch everything: the speaking tube to the engine room and the automatic-pilot gyro; radar screens; the electronic channel selector. The indicator reading STOP—STAND BY—AHEAD and countless other gauges and dials seemed to summon visions of peril on the open sea. In the chart room next door, he gaped at shelves stacked with maps and tables, and studied an erasure-smudged chart still in the drafting. The chart laced the sea with capricious lines which appeared and reappeared according to some curious un-geometry. Most fascinating of all was the daily log: sunrise and sunset were entered as small half-circles, a pair of golden horns marked the passage of the moon, and the ebb and surge of the tides were shown in gentle, rippling curves.

While Noboru wandered through private dreams Tsukazaki stood at Fusako's side, and the heat of his body in the sultry chart room was beginning to oppress her: when the parasol she had leaned against a desk clattered suddenly to the floor, she felt as if she herself, fainting, had fallen.

She raised a little cry. The parasol had glanced off her foot. The sailor stooped immediately and picked it up. To Fusako he seemed to move as slowly as a diver underwater. He retrieved the parasol and then, from the bottom of this sea of breathless time, his white cap rose slowly toward the surface. . . .

Shibuya pushed through the louvered office doors and announced: "Yoriko Kasuga has just arrived."

"All right! I'll be right down."

The old man had revived her too abruptly; she regretted her tinny, reflex reply.

She studied her face for a minute in a mirror hanging on the wall. She felt as if she were still standing in the chart room.

Yoriko was in the patio with one of her ladies-in-waiting. She was wearing a huge sunflower of a hat.

"I want Mama to do all the choosing. I'm just helpless."

Fusako objected to being called "Mama" as though she were the proprietress of a bar. She descended the stairs slowly and walked over to where Yoriko stood chatting.

"And how are you today? It certainly is hot again." The actress complained about the devastating heat and the crowds at the pier where they were filming. Fusako pictured Ryuji somewhere in the throng and her spirits flagged.

"Thirty cuts this morning—can you imagine that? That's what Mr. Honda calls 'racing through a picture.'"

"Will the film be good?"

"Not a chance. But it's not the kind of picture that takes prizes anyway."

Winning a best-actress award had become an obsession with Yoriko. In fact, the gifts she was buying today constituted one of her inimitable "gestures" toward the awards jury. Her willingness to believe any scandal (except one involving herself) suggested that she would proffer her body to every member of the jury without hesitation if she thought that might help.

Though she managed with difficulty to support a family of ten, Yoriko was a gullible beauty and, as Fusako well knew, a very lonely woman. Still, except that she was a good customer, Fusako found her fairly intolerable.

But today Fusako was enveloped in paralyzing gentleness. Yoriko's flaws and her vulgarity were apparent as always, but they seemed as cool and inoffensive as goldfish swimming in a fishbowl.

"At first I thought sweaters might be nice, since it's almost fall, but these are supposed to be things you bought this summer, so I picked out some Caldin ties and some polo shirts and a few Jiff pens. For the wives, I don't think you can go wrong with perfume. Shall we go upstairs? I have everything together in the office."

"I'd love to but I just don't have time. I'll just barely be able to work in a bite of lunch as it is now. Can I leave everything up to you? The important things are the boxes and wrapping—they're the reality of a gift, don't you think?"

"We'll package everything beautifully."

The secretary from Yokohama Importers arrived just as Yoriko was leaving, and she was the last regular customer for the day. Fusako had the sandwich and cup of tea she ordered every day from a coffee shop across the street brought up to her office and sat down in front of the tray alone again. Arranging herself comfortably in the chair like a sleeper burrowing under the covers in an attempt to recapture an interrupted dream, she closed her eyes and returned effortlessly to the bridge of the *Rakuyo*. . . .

Tsukazaki led them down flights of stairs to the boat deck, from where they could watch cargo being raised from the No. 4 hold. The hatch was a large, dark fissure in the steel plates of the deck at their feet. A man in a yellow steel helmet standing on a narrow ledge just below them was directing the crane with hand signals.

The half-naked bodies of stevedores glistened dully in the dusk at the bottom of hold. The cargo first took the sun when it was hoisted wobbling up from the bottom high into the mouth of the hatch. Slats of sunlight slipped nimbly over the crates as they wheeled through the air, but faster even than the shattered light the cargo sped, and was hovering above the waiting barge.

The terrifyingly deliberate prelude and the sudden, reckless flight; the dangerous glitter of silver in a twist of fraying cable—standing under her open parasol, Fusako watched it all. She felt load after heavy load of freight being lifted from her and whisked away on the powerful arm of a crane—suddenly, but after long and careful preparation. She thrilled to the sight of cargo no man could move winging lightly into the sky, and she could have watched forever. This may have been a fitting destiny for cargo but the marvel was also an indignity. "It keeps getting emptier and emptier," she thought. The advance was relentless, yet there was time for hesitation and languor, time so hot and long it made you faint, sluggish, congested time.

She must have spoken then: "It's been so kind of you to show us around when I know you must be very busy. I was wondering, if you're free tomorrow evening, perhaps we could have dinner together?"

It was a sociable invitation and no doubt Fusako spoke the words coolly; to Tsukazaki's ear, it sounded like the babbling of a woman stricken with the heat. He looked at her with perfectly honest, puzzled eyes. . . .

The night before, they had gone to the New Grand Hotel for dinner. *I was still just trying to thank him then. He ate so properly, just like an officer. That long walk after dinner. He said he'd walk me home, but we got to the new park on the hill and didn't feel like saying good night yet, so we sat down on a park bench. Then we had a long talk. Just rambled on about all kinds of things. I've never talked so much with a man before, not since my husband died. . . .*

CHAPTER FOUR

Aｆｔｅｒ leaving Fusako on
her way to work, Ryuji returned briefly to the *Rakuyo*
and then taxied back through empty, simmering streets
to the park where they had stopped the night before.
He couldn't think of anywhere else to go until late
afternoon, when they had arranged to meet.

It was noon and the park was empty. The drinking
fountain was overflowing, dyeing the stone walk a
watery black; locusts were shrilling in the cypress trees.
The harbor, sprawling toward the sea from the foot of
the hill, rumbled thickly. But Ryuji painted out the
noontime scene with reminiscences of night.

He relived the evening, paused to savor a moment,
traced and traced again the night's course. Not bothering to wipe the sweat from his face, he picked absently
at a piece of cigarette paper that clung to his lip while
again and again his mind moaned: *how could I have
talked so goddam badly!*

He hadn't been able to explain his ideas of glory and death, or the longing and the melancholy pent up in his chest, or the other dark passions choking in the ocean's swell. Whenever he tried to talk about those things, he failed. If there were times when he felt he was worthless, there were others when something like the magnificence of the sunset over Manila Bay sent its radiant fire through him and he knew that he had been chosen to tower above other men. But he hadn't been able to tell the woman his conviction. He remembered her asking: "Why haven't you ever married?" And he remembered his simpering answer: "It's not easy to find a woman who is willing to be a sailor's wife."

What he had wanted to say was: "All the other officers have two or three children by now and they read letters from home over and over again, and look at pictures their kids have drawn of houses and the sun and flowers. Those men have thrown opportunity away—there's no hope for them any more. I've never done much, but I've lived my whole life thinking of myself as the only real man. And if I'm right, then a limpid, lonely horn is going to trumpet through the dawn someday, and a turgid cloud laced with light will sweep down, and the poignant voice of glory will call for me from the distance—and I'll have to jump out of bed and set out alone. That's why I've never married. I've waited, and waited, and here I am past thirty."

But he hadn't said anything like that; partly because he doubted a woman would understand. Nor had he mentioned his concept of ideal love: a man encounters the perfect woman only once in a lifetime and in every case death interposes—an unseen Pandarus—and lures them into the preordained embrace. This fantasy was probably a product of the hyperbole of popular songs. But over the years it had taken on substance in some recess of his mind and merged there with other things: the shrieking of a tidal wave, the ineluctable force of high tide, the avalanching break of surf upon a shoal. . . .

And he had been certain that the woman before him was the woman in the dream. If only he had found the words to say it.

In the grand dream Ryuji had treasured secretly for so long, he was a paragon of manliness and she the consummate woman; and from the opposite corners of the earth they came together in a chance encounter, and death wed them. Outdistancing tawdry farewells then, with streamers waving and strains of "Auld Lang Syne," and far from sailors' fickle loves, they were to descend to the bottom of the heart's great deep where no man has ever been. . . .

But he hadn't been able to share even a fragment of his mad dream. Instead, he had talked of greens: "Every once in a while when you're on a long cruise and you pass the galley you catch just a glimpse of radish or maybe turnip leaves. And you know, those little splashes of green make you tingle all over. You feel like getting down on your knees and worshipping them."

"I can imagine. I think I know just how you must feel." Fusako agreed eagerly. Her voice oozed the joy a woman takes in consoling a man.

Ryuji asked for her fan and shooed the mosquitoes away. Lamps on distant masts twinkled like ocher stars; bulbs in the eaves of the warehouses directly below stretched in regular, bright rows.

He wanted to talk about the strange passion that catches hold of a man by the scruff of his neck and transports him to a realm beyond the fear of death. But far from finding words for that, he volunteered an account of the hardships he had known, and clucked his tongue.

His father, a civil servant, had raised him and his sister singlehanded after their mother's death; the sickly old man had worked overtime in order to send Ryuji to school; despite everything, Ryuji had grown up into a strong, healthy man; late in the war his home had been destroyed in an air raid and his sister had died of typhus shortly after; he had graduated from the merchant-marine high school and was just starting on his career when his father died too; his only memories of life on shore were of poverty and sickness and death, of endless devastation; by becoming a sailor, he had detached himself from the land forever. . . . It was the first time he had talked of these things at such length to a woman.

Exaltation swelled Ryuji's voice when he touched on the misery in his life, and while he was recalling the total in his bankbook he couldn't help digressing from the sea's power and benevolence, which was the story he had longed to tell, in order to boast about his own prowess like a very ordinary man indeed. It was just another particular aspect of his vanity.

He wanted to talk about the sea—he might have said something like this: "It was the sea that made me begin thinking secretly about love more than anything else; you know, a love worth dying for, or a love that consumes you. To a man locked up in a steel ship all the time, the sea is too much like a woman. Things like her lulls and storms, or her caprice, or the beauty of her breast reflecting the setting sun, are all obvious. More than that, you're in a ship that mounts the sea and rides her and yet is constantly denied her. It's the old saw about miles and miles of lovely water and you can't quench your thirst. Nature surrounds a sailor with all these elements so like a woman and yet he is kept as far as a man can be from her warm, living body. That's where the problem begins, right there—I'm sure of it."

But he could only mouth a few lines of his song:

Now the sea's my home, I decided that. But even I must shed a tear . . . "I guess that's pretty funny. It's my favorite song."

"I think it's a wonderful song," she said. But she was only shielding his pride, he knew. Obviously this was the first time she had ever heard the song, though she pretended to know it well. *She can't penetrate to the feelings deep down in a song like this; or see through the murk of my manhood to the longing that sometimes makes me weep; fair enough: then as far as I'm concerned, she's just another body.*

He saw at a glance how delicate and how fragrant a body it was.

Fusako was wearing a black-lace kimono over a crimson under-robe, and her obi was white brocade. Her milky face floated coolly in the dusk. Crimson peeped seductively through the black lace. She was a presence suffusing the air around them with the softness of being a woman; an extravagant, elegant woman —Ryuji had never seen anything like her.

The robe shifted fantastically from crimson through shades of purple as every subtle movement of her body altered the play of light from the distant lamps; and he detected within the shadowed folds of cloth the hushed breathing of the woman's own folds. Her sweat and perfume fragrance reaching him on the breeze seemed to clamor for his death. "DIE! DIE! DIE!" it screamed; and he imagined the time when her delicate fingertips, stealthy now and reluctant, would quicken into tongues of flame.

Her nose was perfect; her lips exquisite. Like a master ringing a *go* stone onto the board after long deliberation, he placed the details of her beauty one by one in the misty dark and drew back to savor them.

Her eyes were quiet, and icy, and their chill was lewdness itself, indifference to the world become reckless lechery. Her eyes had haunted Ryuji since they had agreed to meet for dinner the day before; they had kept him awake all night.

And what voluptuous shoulders! Like the shoreline, they began with no real beginning, to slope gently downward from the cape of her neck; gracious, dignified shoulders fashioned so that silk might slip and fall away. *When I hold her breasts they'll nestle against my palms with a marvelous, sweaty heaviness. I feel responsible for all this woman's flesh because it teases me softly like other things that are mine. I'm trembling with the sweetness of her being here, and when she feels me tremble she'll tilt up like a leaf in a wind-tossed tree and show the white backs of those eyes of hers.*

An odd, silly story thrust abruptly into Ryuji's mind. Once the Captain had told him about going to Venice and visiting a beautiful little palace at high tide; and being astounded to find when he got there that the marble floors were under water. . . . Ryuji almost spoke the words aloud: *small beautiful flooded palace.*

"Please talk some more," Fusako begged, and he knew it would be all right to kiss her. The smooth, inflamed play of their lips altered subtly with every contact and clinging release as from angle after angle they poured each other full of light, spinning into a single luminous thread all of softness and of sweetness. The shoulders under his rough hands now were more real than any dream.

Like an insect folding in its wings, Fusako lowered her long lashes. Happiness enough to drive a man crazy, Ryuji thought. Happiness that defied description. At first Fusako's breath seemed to climb from somewhere in her chest, but gradually its heat and odor changed until it might have issued from some unfathomable depth within her. Now the fuel firing her breath was different too.

They clutched at each other and collided in frenzied, awkward movements like beasts in a forest lunging at a ring of fire. Fusako's lips softened and became smoother; Ryuji was ready to die happily that very moment. Only when the cool tips of their noses brushed did he realize with a chuckle that they were two firm, separate bodies.

He didn't know how much time passed before, pointing toward a slate roof jutting above the cypress trees at the edge of the park, she said: "Why don't you stay with us tonight? That's our house over there."

They stood up and looked around. Ryuji jammed his

cap on his head and put his arm around Fusako's shoulders. The park was empty; the red-and-green beacon in the Marine Tower swept across stone benches in the empty square, the drinking fountain, flower beds, and white stone steps.

Out of habit, Ryuji glanced at his watch. He could just see the dial in the light from the street lamp outside the park: a few minutes past ten. Ordinarily, he would have two hours until night watch. . . .

He couldn't take any more of the noonday heat. The sun was in the west now, frying the back of his head: he had left his cap on the *Rakuyo*.

The First Mate had given Ryuji a two-day leave, assigning his watch to the Third Mate with the understanding that Ryuji would stand in for him at the next port. He had changed clothes on the ship and had with him a sport jacket and tie he planned to wear that evening, but already sweat had bedraggled his dress shirt.

He looked at his watch. It was only four o'clock. His date with Fusako was for six. The coffee shop where they had arranged to meet apparently had color television—but there wouldn't be anything interesting on at this hour of the day.

Ryuji walked over to the park railing and looked out at the harbor. The warehouse roofs below were extending their three-cornered shadows toward the foreshore. One white sail was tacking back to the yacht basin. He watched the sun sculpture a brace of tensed muscles in marvelous detail in the snow-white blocks of cloud piled above the offing. They were storm clouds all right, but not swollen enough for an evening squall.

The memory of a mischievous game he had often played as a child drew him across the lawn to the drinking fountain. Closing the mouth of the fountain with his thumb, he squirted a fan of water at the dahlias and white chrysanthemums languishing in the heat: leaves quivered, a small rainbow arched, flowers recoiled. Ryuji reversed the pressure of his thumb and doused his hair and face and throat. The water trickled from his throat to his chest and belly, spinning a soft, cooling screen—an indescribable delight.

Ryuji shook himself all over like a dog and, carrying his sport jacket over his arm, moved toward the entrance of the park. His shirt was drenched but he didn't bother to take it off: the sun would dry it quickly enough.

Ryuji left the park. He marveled at the serenity of the houses that lined the streets, at the sturdy roofs and rooted, unbudging fences. As always, the details of shore life appeared abstract and unreal. Even when he passed an open kitchen and glimpsed the glitter of polished pots and pans, everything lacked concreteness. His sexual desires too, the more so because they were physical, he apprehended as pure abstraction; lusts which time had relegated to memory remained only as glistening essences, like salt crystallized at the surface of a compound. *We'll go to bed together again tonight —this one's the last: we probably won't sleep at all. I sail tomorrow evening. I wouldn't be surprised if I evaporated faster than a damn memory, thanks to these two fantastic nights. . . .*

The heat wasn't making him sleepy. But imagination whetted his lust as he walked along and he narrowly avoided a large foreign car that came roaring up the hill.

Then he saw a group of boys break onto the main road from a footpath near the bottom of the hill. Seeing him, one of them stopped short—it was Noboru. Ryuji noticed the boyish kneecaps below the shorts tighten abruptly, saw tension cramp the face peering up at him; and he recalled what Fusako had said: *There was something about Noboru this morning; almost as if he knew. . . .* Battling with a part of himself that threatened to be flustered in front of the boy, Ryuji forced a smile and yelled: "Hey! Small world, isn't it? Have a good swim?" The boy didn't answer; his clear, dispassionate gaze was fixed on Ryuji's shirt.

"Why—how did your shirt get sopped like that?"

"What, this?" The artificial smile spread over his face again. "I took a little shower at the fountain up there in the park."

CHAPTER FIVE

Rᴜɴɴɪɴɢ into Ryuji near the park worried Noboru. He wondered what he could do to keep the sailor from telling his mother about the meeting. In the first place, he hadn't gone swimming at Kamakura as the adults supposed. Besides, one of the boys in the group Ryuji had seen was the chief. But that wasn't so bad. No one would be able to tell him from the others just by looking—not a chance.

That morning, the boys had left the city with packed lunches and gone all the way to Yamauchi Pier in Kanagawa. For a while they had roamed around the railroad siding behind the sheds on the wharf, and then held the usual meeting to discuss the uselessness of Mankind, the insignificance of Life. They liked an insecure meeting place where intrusion was always a possibility.

The chief, number one, number two, Noboru (who was number three), number four, and number five were all smallish, delicate boys and excellent students. In fact most of their teachers lavished praise on this outstanding group and even held it up as an encouraging example to poorer students.

Number two had discovered that morning's meeting place and all the others had approved. In back of a large shed marked "City Maintenance A" a rusty railroad siding, apparently in long disuse, crawled through high wild chrysanthemums and old abandoned tires across an unkempt field. Far away in the small garden in front of the warehouse office, canna flowers were blazing in the sun. They were dwindling, end-of-summer flames, but so long as they were visible the boys didn't feel free of the watchman's eye, so they turned away and followed the siding back from the shed. The track stopped in front of a black heavily bolted warehouse door. They discovered to one side of the warehouse a patch of grass hidden by a high wall of red and yellow and deep-brown drums, and sat down. The garish sun was edging toward the summit of the roof but the little lawn was still in shade.

"That sailor is terrific! He's like a fantastic beast that's just come out of the sea all dripping wet. Last night I watched him go to bed with my mother."

Noboru began an excited account of what he had witnessed the night before. The boys kept their faces blank, but he could feel every eye on him and the straining to catch every word, and he was satisfied.

"And that's your hero?" the chief said when he had finished. His thin red upper lip had a tendency to curl when he spoke. "Don't you realize there is no such thing as a hero in this world?"

"But he's different. He's really going to do something."

"Oh? Like what, for instance?"

"I can't say exactly, but it'll be something . . . terrific."

"Are you kidding? A guy like that never does anything. He's probably after your old lady's money; that'll be the punch line. First he'll suck her out of everything she's got and then, bang, bam, see you around, ma'am—that'll be the punch line."

"Well even that's something isn't it? Something we couldn't do?"

"Your ideas about people are still pretty naïve," the thirteen-year-old chief said coldly. "No adult is going to be able to do something we couldn't do. There's a huge seal called 'impossibility' pasted all over this world. And don't ever forget that we're the only ones who can tear it off once and for all." Awe-stricken, the others fell silent.

"How about your folks?" the chief asked, turning to number two. "I suppose they still won't buy you an air rifle?"

"Naw—I guess it's hopeless," the boy crooned to himself, arms hugging his knees.

"They probably say it would be dangerous, don't they?"

"Yes. . . ."

"That's crap!" Dimples dented the chief's cheeks, white even in summer. "They don't even know the definition of danger. They think danger means something physical, getting scratched and a little blood running and the newspapers making a big fuss. Well, that hasn't got anything to do with it. Real danger is nothing more than just living. Of course, living is merely the chaos of existence, but more than that it's a crazy mixed-up business of dismantling existence instant by instant to the point where the original chaos is restored, and taking strength from the uncertainty and the fear that chaos brings to re-create existence instant by instant. You won't find another job as dangerous as that. There isn't any fear in existence itself, or any uncertainty, but living creates it. And society is basically meaningless, a Roman mixed bath. And school, school is just society in miniature: that's why we're always being ordered around. A bunch of blind men tell us what to do, tear our unlimited ability to shreds."

"But how about the sea?" Noboru persisted. "How about a ship? Last night I'm sure I caught the meaning of the internal order of life you talked about."

"I suppose the sea is permissible to a certain extent." The chief took a deep breath of the salt breeze blowing in between the sheds. "As a matter of fact, it's probably more permissible than any of the few other permissible things. I don't know about a ship, though. I don't see why a ship is any different from a car."

"Because you don't understand."

"Is that right? . . ." An expression of chagrin at this blow to his pride appeared between the chief's thin, crescent-shaped eyebrows. Their artificial look, as though they were painted on, was the barber's fault: he insisted, despite the chief's protestations, on shaving his brow and above his eyelids. "Is that right? Since when is it your place to tell me what I understand and what I don't?"

"C'mon, let's eat." Number five was a quiet, gentle boy.

They had just unwrapped their lunches on their laps when Noboru noticed a shadow fall across the lawn and looked up in surprise. The old watchman from the warehouse, his elbows propped on a drum, was peering in at them.

"You boys sure picked a messy place for a picnic." With admirable poise, the chief beamed a scrubbed, schoolboy smile at the old man and said: "Would it be better for us to go somewhere else? We came down to watch the ships, and then we were looking for a shady place to have lunch. . . ."

"Go right ahead; you're not doing any harm. Just be sure not to leave any litter around."

"Yes, sir." The smiles were boyish, innocent. "You don't have to worry about that—we're hungry enough to eat the wrappings and everything, right, you guys?"

They watched the hunchback shuffle down the path, treading the border between sunlight and shadow. Number four was the first to speak: "There are plenty of that type around—about as common as you can get, and he just loves 'the youngsters.' I'll bet he felt so generous just now."

The boys shared the sandwiches and raw vegetables and little cakes in their lunches and drank iced tea from small thermos bottles. A few sparrows flew in over the siding and alighted just outside their circle, but no one shared even a crumb with the birds. Matchless inhumanity was a point of pride with every one of them.

These were children from "good homes," and their mothers had packed them rich and varied lunches: Noboru was a little ashamed of the plainish sandwiches he had brought. They sat cross-legged on the ground, some in shorts, some in dungarees. The chief's throat labored painfully as he wolfed his food.

It was very hot. Now the sun was flaming directly above the warehouse roof, the shallow eaves barely protecting them.

Noboru munched his food in nervous haste, a habit his mother often scolded him for, squinting upward into the glare as he ate as if to catch the sun in his open mouth. He was recalling the design of the perfect painting he had seen the night before. It had been almost a manifestation of the absolutely blue sky of night. The chief maintained that there was nothing new to be found anywhere in the world, but Noboru still believed in the adventure lurking in some tropical backland. And he believed in the many-colored market at the hub of clamor and confusion in some distant seaport, in the bananas and parrots sold from the glistening arms of black natives.

"You're daydreaming while you eat, aren't you? That's a child's habit." Noboru didn't answer; he wasn't equal to the scorn in the chief's voice. Besides, he reasoned, getting mad would only look silly because they were practicing "absolute dispassion."

Noboru had been trained in such a way that practically nothing sexual, not even that scene the night before, could surprise him. The chief had taken great pains to insure that none of the gang would be abashed by such a sight. Somehow he had managed to obtain photographs picturing intercourse in every conceivable position and a remarkable selection of pre-coital techniques, and explained them all in detail, warmly instructing the boys about the insignificance, the unworthiness of such activity.

Ordinarily a boy with merely a physical edge on his classmates presides at lessons such as these, but the chief's case was altogether different: he appealed directly to the intellect. To begin with, he maintained that their genitals were for copulating with stars in the Milky Way. Their pubic hair, indigo roots buried deep beneath white skin and a few strands already strong and thickening, would grow out in order to tickle coy stardust when the rape occurred. . . . This kind of hallowed raving enchanted them and they disdained their classmates, foolish, dirty, pitiful boys brimming with curiosity about sex.

"When we finish eating we'll go over to my place," the chief said. "Everything's all ready for you know what."

"Got a cat?"

"Not yet, but it won't take long to find one. Nothing will take long."

Since the chief's house was near Noboru's, they had to take a train again to get there: the boys liked this sort of unnecessary, troublesome excursion.

The chief's parents were never home; his house was always hushed. A solitary boy, he had read at thirteen every book in the house and was always bored. He claimed he could tell what any book was about just by looking at the cover.

There were indications that this hollow house had nourished the chief's ideas about the overwhelming emptiness of the world. Noboru had never seen so many entrances and exits, so many prim chilly rooms. The house even made him afraid to go to the bathroom alone: foghorns in the harbor echoed emptily from room to empty room.

Sometimes, ushering the boys into his father's study and sitting down in front of a handsome morocco-leather desk set, the chief would write out topics for discussion, moving his pen importantly between ink-well and copper-engraved stationery. Whenever he made a mistake, he would crumple the thick imported paper and toss it carelessly away. Once Noboru had asked: "Won't your old man get mad if you do that?" The chief had rewarded him with silence and a derisive smile.

But they all loved a large shed in the garden in back where they could go without passing under the butler's eye. Except for a few logs and some shelves full of tools and empty wine bottles and back issues of foreign magazines, the floor of the shed was bare, and when they sat down on the damp dark earth its coolness passed directly to their buttocks.

After hunting for an hour, they found a stray cat small enough to ride in the palm of Noboru's hand, a mottled, mewing kitten with lackluster eyes.

By then they were sweating heavily, so they undressed and took turns splashing in a sink in one corner of the shed. While they bathed, the kitten was passed around. Noboru felt the kitten's hot heart pumping against his wet naked chest. It was like having stolen into the shed with some of the dark, joy-flushed essence of bright summer sunlight.

"How are we going to do it?"

"There's a log over there. We can smack it against that—it'll be easy. Go ahead, number three."

At last the test of Noboru's hard, cold heart! Just a minute before, he had taken a cold bath, but he was sweating heavily again. He felt it blow up through his breast like the morning sea breeze: intent to kill. His chest felt like a clothes rack made of hollow metal poles and hung with white shirts drying in the sun. Soon the shirts would be flapping in the wind and then he would be killing, breaking the endless chain of society's loathsome taboos.

Noboru seized the kitten by the neck and stood up. It dangled dumbly from his fingers. He checked himself for pity; like a lighted window seen from an express train, it flickered for an instant in the distance and disappeared. He was relieved.

The chief always insisted it would take acts such as this to fill the world's great hollows. Though nothing else could do it, he said, murder would fill those gaping caves in much the same way that a crack along its face will fill a mirror. Then they would achieve real power over existence.

Resolved, Noboru swung the kitten high above his

head and slammed it at the log. The warm soft thing hurtled through the air in marvelous flight. But the sensation of down between his fingers lingered.

"It's not dead yet. Do it again," the chief ordered.

Scattered through the gloom in the shed, the five naked boys stood rooted, their eyes glittering.

What Noboru lifted between two fingers now was no longer a kitten. A resplendent power was surging through him to the tips of his fingers and he had only to lift the dazzling arc seared into the air by this power and hurl it again and again at the log. He felt like a giant of a man. Just once, at the second impact, the kitten raised a short, gurgling cry. . . .

The kitten had bounced off the log for the final time. Its hind legs twitched, traced large lax circles in the dirt floor, and then subsided. The boys were overjoyed at the spattered blood on the log.

As if staring into a deep well, Noboru peered after the kitten as it plummeted down the small hole of death. He sensed in the way he lowered his face to the corpse his own gallant tenderness, tenderness so clinical it was almost kind. Dull red blood oozed from the kitten's nose and mouth, the twisted tongue was clamped against the palate.

"C'mon up close where you can see. I'll take it from here." Unnoticed, the chief had put on a pair of rubber gloves that reached up to his elbows; now he bent over the corpse with a pair of gleaming scissors. Shining coolly through the gloom of the shed, the scissors were magnificent in their cold, intellectual dignity: Noboru couldn't imagine a more appropriate weapon for the chief.

Seizing the kitten by the neck, the chief pierced the skin at the chest with the point of the blade and scissored a long smooth cut to the throat. Then he pushed the skin to the sides with both hands: the glossy layer of fat beneath was like a peeled spring onion. The skinned neck, draped gracefully on the floor, seemed to be wearing a cat mask. The cat was only an exterior, life had posed as a cat.

But beneath the surface was a smooth expression-less interior, a placid, glossy-white inner life in perfect consonance with Noboru and the others; and they could feel their own intricate, soot-black insides bear-ing down upon and shadowing it like ships moving upon the water. Now, at last, the boys and the cat, or, more accurately, what had been a cat, became per-fectly at one.

Gradually the endoderm was bared; its transparent mother-of-pearl loveliness was not at all repellent. They could see through to the ribs now, and watch, beneath the great omentum, the warm, homey pulsing of the colon.

"What do you think? Doesn't it look too naked? I'm

not sure that's such a good thing: like it was bad manners or something." The chief peeled aside the skin on the trunk with his gloved hands.

"It sure is naked," said number two.

Noboru tried comparing the corpse confronting the world so nakedly with the unsurpassably naked figures of his mother and the sailor. But compared to this, they weren't naked enough. They were still swaddled in skin. Even that marvelous horn and the great wide world whose expanse it had limned couldn't possibly have penetrated so deeply as this . . . the pumping of the bared heart placed the peeled kitten in direct and tingling contact with the kernel of the world.

Noboru wondered, pressing a crumpled handkerchief to his nose against the mounting stench and breathing hotly through his mouth: "What is beginning here now?"

The kitten bled very little. The chief tore through the surrounding membrane and exposed the large, red-black liver. Then he unwound the immaculate bowels and reeled them onto the floor. Steam rose and nestled against the rubber gloves. He cut the colon into slices and squeezed out for all the boys to see a broth the color of lemons. "This stuff cuts just like flannel."

Noboru managed, while following his own dreamy thoughts, to pay scrupulous attention to the details. The kitten's dead pupils were purple flecked with white; the gaping mouth was stuffed with congealed

blood, the twisted tongue visible between the fangs. As
the fat-yellowed scissors cut them, he heard the ribs
creak. And he watched intently while the chief groped
in the abdominal cavity, withdrew the small pericar-
dium, and plucked from it the tiny oval heart. When he
squeezed the heart between two fingers, the remaining
blood gushed onto his rubber gloves, reddening them to
the tips of the fingers.

What is really happening here?

Noboru had withstood the ordeal from beginning to
end. Now his half-dazed brain envisioned the warmth
of the scattered viscera and the pools of blood in the
gutted belly finding wholeness and perfection in
the rapture of the dead kitten's large languid soul. The
liver, limp beside the corpse, became a soft peninsula,
the squashed heart a little sun, the reeled-out bowels a
white atoll, and the blood in the belly the tepid waters
of a tropical sea. Death had transfigured the kitten into
a perfect, autonomous world.

I killed it all by myself—a distant hand reached into
Noboru's dream and awarded him a snow-white certifi-
cate of merit—*I can do anything, no matter how awful.*

The chief peeled off the squeaky rubber gloves and
laid one beautiful white hand on Noboru's shoulder.
"You did a good job. I think we can say this has finally
made a real man of you—and isn't all this blood a sight
for sore eyes!"

CHAPTER SIX

MEETING Ryuji on the
way back from the chief's house just after they had
buried the cat was pure bad luck. Noboru had
scrubbed his hands, but what if there was blood somewhere else on his body or on his clothes? What if he
reeked of dead kitten? What if his eyes betrayed him—
like those of a criminal encountering an acquaintance
just after the crime?

For one thing, there would be trouble if his mother
learned that he had been near the park at this time of
day: he was supposed to be in Kamakura with a different group of friends. Noboru had been caught off
guard, he was even a little frightened, and he decided
arbitrarily that Ryuji was entirely to blame.

The others scattered after hurried goodbyes and
they were left alone on the hot road with their long
afternoon shadows.

Noboru was mortified. He had been waiting for an opening to introduce Ryuji casually. If, under perfect circumstances, the introduction had succeeded, the chief might have admitted reluctantly that Ryuji was a hero and Noboru's honor would have been redeemed.

But at this unhappy, unexpected meeting, the sailor had presented himself as a pitiful figure in a water-logged shirt and, as if that wasn't enough, smiled like a fawning idiot. That smile was a disparagement, for it was meant to mollify a child; besides, it transformed Ryuji himself into a disgraceful caricature of the adult lover of youngsters. Overbright and artificial, an unnecessary, outrageous blunder of a smile!

On top of that, Ryuji had said things he should never have said: "Small world, isn't it? Have a good swim?" And when Noboru challenged the soaking shirt, he should have answered: "Oh, this? I rescued a woman who had thrown herself off the pier. This makes the third time I've had to go swimming with all my clothes on. . . ."

But he hadn't said anything of the kind. Instead he had offered this ridiculous explanation: "I took a little shower at the fountain up there in the park." And with that unwarranted smile all over his face!

He wants me to like him. I guess having your new woman's brat kid like you can be pretty convenient at times.

They found themselves walking in the direction of

the house. Ryuji, who still had two hours on his hands, fell into step with the boy, feeling pleased to have found someone to pass the time with. "There's something funny about both of us today," he volunteered as they walked along.

Noboru didn't like the show of eager sympathy, but it made asking an important favor easy: "Mr. Tsukazaki, would you mind not telling Mom about seeing me at the park?"

"You bet."

The sailor's pleasure at being entrusted with a secret, his reassuring smile and quick assent, disappointed Noboru. At least he could have threatened a little.

"I'm supposed to have been at the beach all day—just a minute." Noboru sprinted to a sand pile at the side of the road and, kicking off his tennis shoes, began to rub his feet and legs with handfuls of sand. The smug, affected boy moved with an animal quickness Ryuji hadn't seen before. Conscious of being watched, Noboru was putting on a show, smearing the sand on the backs of his legs and all the way up his thighs. When he was satisfied, he stepped into his shoes gingerly so as not to dislodge the sand and minced back to Ryuji. "Look," he said, indicating the sand on his sweating thigh, "it stuck in the shape of a draftsman's curve."

"Where are you headed now?"

"Home. Why don't you come too, Mr. Tsukazaki?

There's an air conditioner in the living room and it's really cool."

They turned on the air conditioner and Ryuji slumped into a rattan chair. Noboru, after returning from an artfully reluctant trip to the bathroom under orders from the housekeeper to wash his feet, sprawled on the rattan couch near the closed window.

The housekeeper came in with cool drinks and began to scold again: "I'm going to tell your mother just how bad you behave in front of company—flopping all over the place like that."

Noboru's eyes sought help from Ryuji.

"It doesn't bother me a bit. And swimming all day does seem to have tired him out."

"I suppose so—but he should know better. . . ."

Obviously the housekeeper resented Ryuji and she appeared to be venting her disgruntlement on Noboru. Heaving from side to side buttocks heavy with discontent, she lumbered out of the room.

Ryuji's defense had united them in a tacit pact. Noboru swilled his drink, dribbling yellow fruit juice on his throat. Then he turned to look at the sailor, and, for the first time, his eyes were smiling. "I know just about everything when it comes to ships."

"You'd probably put an old pro like me to shame."

"I don't like to be flattered." Noboru raised his head from a cushion his mother had embroidered; for an instant, there was fury in his eyes.

"What time do you stand watch, Mr. Tsukazaki?"

"From noon to four and from midnight to four. That's why they call it 'thieves' watch.'"

"Thieves' watch! Boy, that sounds great!" This time Noboru laughed outright and arched his back into a bow.

"How many men stand watch together?"

"A duty officer and two helmsmen."

"Mr. Tsukazaki, how much does a ship list in a squall?"

"Thirty to forty degrees when it gets really bad. Try walking up a forty-degree grade sometime. It's like scaling a damn wall—fantastic. There are times when . . ."

Groping for words, Ryuji stared into space. Noboru saw in his eyes the billows of a storm-riled sea and felt mildly seasick. He was ecstatic.

"The *Rakuyo* is a tramp steamer, isn't she, Mr. Tsukazaki?"

"Yes, that's right," Ryuji admitted halfheartedly: his pride was hurt a little.

"I guess most of your routes are between Japan and China and then India, right?"

"You do know what you're talking about, don't you? Sometimes we ship wheat from Australia to England too."

Noboru's questions were precipitate, his interest

leaped from one subject to another. "What was the Philippines' chief product again?"

"Lauan wood, I guess."

"How about Malaya?"

"That'd be iron ore. Here's one for you: what's Cuba's chief product?"

"Sugar. What else? Anybody knows that. Say, have you ever been to the West Indies?"

"Yes. Just once, though."

"Did you get to Haiti?"

"Yes."

"Boy! How about the trees there?"

"Trees?"

"You know, like shade trees or—"

"Oh, that—palms mostly. And then the mountains are full of what they call flamboyants. And silk trees. I can't remember whether the flamboyant looks like the silk tree or not. Anyway, when they blossom, they look like they're on fire. And when the sky gets pitch black just before an evening storm they turn fantastic colors. I've never seen blossoms like that again anywhere."

Ryuji wanted to talk about his mysterious attachment to a grove of wine palms. But he didn't know how to tell that kind of story to a child, and as he sat and wondered, the doomsday glow of sunset in the Persian Gulf roused in his mind, and the sea wind caressing his cheek as he stood at the anchor davit, and the rankling fall of the barometer that warned of an approaching typhoon: he was sensible again of the sea's nightmarish power working endlessly on his moods, his passions.

Noboru, just as he had seen storm billows a minute before, beheld one by one in the sailor's eyes the phantoms he had summoned. Surrounded by visions of distant lands and by white-paint nautical jargon, he was being swept away to the Gulf of Mexico, the Indian Ocean, the Persian Gulf. And the journey was made possible by this authentic Second Mate. Here at last was the medium without which his imagination had been helpless. How long he had waited for it!

Rapturous, Noboru shut his eyes tight.

The two-horsepower motor in the air conditioner whispered to the room. It was perfectly cool now, and Ryuji's shirt had dried. He clasped his rough hands behind his head: the ridges in the finely laced rattan nestled coolly against his fingers.

His eyes roved the dim room and he marveled at the golden clock enthroned on the mantel, the cut-glass chandelier depending from the ceiling, the graceful jade vases poised precariously on open shelves: all delicate, all absolutely still. He wondered what subtle providence kept the room from rocking. Until a day before, the objects here had meant nothing to him, and in a day he would be gone; yet, for the moment, they were connected. The link was a glance met by a woman's eyes, a signal emanating from deep in the flesh, the brute power of his own manhood; and to know this filled him with a sense of mystery, as when he sighted an unknown vessel on the open sea. Though his own flesh had fashioned the bond, its enormous unreality with respect to this room made him tremble.

What am I supposed to be doing here on a summer afternoon? Who am I, sitting in a daze next to the son of a woman I made last night? Until yesterday I had my song—"the sea's my home, I decided that"—and the tears I cried for it, and two million yen in my bank account as guarantees of my reality—what have I got now?

Noboru didn't realize that Ryuji was sinking into a void. He didn't even notice that the sailor wasn't looking in his direction any more. Lack of sleep and a succession of shocks had exhausted him, the bloodshot eyes he had told the housekeeper were from the salt water were beginning to close. He pondered, as he rocked toward sleep, the glistening figures of absolute reality twice glimpsed since the night before during lapses in the unmoving, tedious, barren world. . . .

He saw them as marvelous gold embroideries leaping off a flat black fabric: the naked sailor twisting in the moonlight to confront a horn—the kitten's death mask, grave and fang-bared—its ruby heart . . . gorgeous entities all and absolutely authentic: then Ryuji too was an authentic hero . . . all incidents on the sea, in the sea, under the sea—Noboru felt himself drowning in sleep. "Happiness," he thought. "Happiness that defies description. . . ." He fell asleep.

Ryuji looked at his watch: it was time to go. He knocked lightly on the door leading to the kitchen and called the housekeeper.

"He's fallen asleep."

"That's just like that boy."

"He might catch a chill. If there's a blanket or something—"

"I'll get one from upstairs."

"Well—I'll be going now."

"I suppose we can expect you back tonight?" A smirk appeared around the housekeeper's eyes and trickled down her face as she glanced once, quickly, ogling up at Ryuji.

CHAPTER SEVEN

SINCE dark antiquity the words have been spoken by women of every caste to sailors in every port; words of docile acceptance of the horizon's authority, of reckless homage to that mysterious azure boundary; words never failing to bestow on even the haughtiest woman the sadness, the hollow hopes, and the freedom of the whore: "You'll be leaving in the morning, won't you? . . ."

But Fusako was determined not to submit, though she knew Ryuji would try to make her speak. She understood that he was staking a simple man's pride on the tears of a woman lamenting the farewell. And what a simple man he was! Their conversation in the park the night before was proof of that. First he had misled her with his pensive look into expecting profound observations or even a passionate declaration, and then he had begun a monologue on shreds of green leaf, and prattled about his personal history, and finally, horribly entangled in his own story, burst into the refrain of a popular song!

Yet she was relieved to know that he was not a dreamer, and his plainness, a quality more durable than imaginative, like a piece of sturdy old furniture, she found reassuring. Fusako needed a guarantee of safety, for she had pampered herself too long, avoided danger in any form, and her unexpected and dangerous actions since the night before had frightened her. Feeling up in the air as she did, it seemed vitally important that the man with whom she was involved be down-to-earth. There were still things to learn of course, but at least she was convinced that Ryuji was not the sort of man to burden her financially.

On their way to a steakhouse at the Bashado, they passed a little café with a fountain in the garden and small red and yellow lights strung along the awning over the entrance, and decided to go in for a drink before dinner.

For some reason, the mint frappé Fusako ordered was garnished with a cherry, stem and all. She deftly tore the fruit away with her teeth and placed the pit in a shallow glass ashtray.

The glow that lingered in the sky was sifting through the lace curtains on the large front window, suffusing the almost empty room. It must have been due to those delicately tinted rays of light: the smooth, warm cherry pit, just perceptibly beginning to dry and ineffably pink, appeared incredibly seductive to Ryuji. He reached for it abruptly and put it into his mouth. A cry of surprise rose to Fusako's lips, then she began to laugh. She had never known a moment of such peaceful physical intimacy.

They chose a quiet neighborhood for a walk after dinner. Captives of a tenderness that might have bewitched the summer night, they walked in silence, holding hands. Fusako brushed at her hair with her free hand. That afternoon she had watched for a lull in business at the shop, then dashed to the beauty parlor for a quick hairdo. Remembering the puzzlement on the beautician's face when she had declined the perfumed oil she always had her comb lightly through her hair, Fusako blushed. Now her whole body threatened to unravel into a sloppy heap amid the smells of the city and the summer night.

Tomorrow, the thick fingers twined in her own would plunge over the horizon It was unbelievable, like a ridiculous, spectacular lie. Fusako blurted, as they were passing a nursery that had closed for the day: "I've sunk pretty low thanks to you."

"Why?" Surprised, Ryuji stopped.

Fusako peered through the wire fence at the trees and shrubbery and rose bushes all tightly packed together in the nursery garden. It was pitch dark, the luxuriant foliage was unnaturally tangled and involuted: she felt suddenly as though a terrible eye were looking into her.

"Why?" Ryuji asked again; Fusako didn't answer. As the mistress of a respectable shore household, she wanted to protest being forced into a pattern of life which began with waving goodbye to a man, a pattern familiar to any harbor whore. But that would have been only one step away from giving utterance to those other words: you'll be leaving in the morning, won't you? . . .

A solitary life aboard ship had taught Ryuji not to probe matters he didn't understand. Fusako's complaint he interpreted as typical, a woman whining: his second "why" was therefore playful, teasing. The thought of parting with her the next day was painful, but he had a maxim to countermand his pain, an insubstantial refrain which played over and over in his dreams: "The man sets out in quest of the Grand Cause; the woman is left behind." Yet Ryuji knew better than anyone that no Grand Cause was to be found at sea. At sea were only watches linking night and day, prosaic tedium, the wretched circumstances of a prisoner.

And the admonishing cables: "Recently vessels of this line have been plagued by a succession of collisions in the Irako Channel and at the northern entrance to Kijima Straits stop request extreme caution in narrow channels and harbor entrances stop in view of this line's current situation request redoubled efforts to eliminate all accidents at sea stop Director of Maritime Shipping." The cliché "in view of this line's current situation" had been included in every wordy cable since the beginning of the so-called shipping slump.

And the Quartermaster's log, a daily record of weather, wind velocity, atmospheric pressure, temperature, relative humidity, speed, distance logged, and revolutions per minute, a diary accurately recording the sea's caprice in compensation for man's inability to chart his own moods.

And, in the mess room, traditional dancing dolls, five portholes, a map of the world on the wall. The soy-sauce bottle was suspended from the ceiling on a leather strap: sometimes round bars of sunlight lanced toward the bottle and slipped back, darted in again as if to lap the lurching, tea-brown liquid, then withdrew again. Posted on the galley wall was an ostentatiously lettered breakfast menu:

> Miso Soup with Eggplant and Bean Curd
> Stewed White Radishes
> Raw Onions, Mustard, Rice

Lunch was Western style and always began with soup.

And the green engine, tossing and moaning inside its twisted tubes like the feverish victim of a fatal disease. . . .

In a day, all this would become Ryuji's world again.

They had stopped in front of a small gate in the

nursery fence. Ryuji's shoulder brushed against the gate and it clicked open, swinging in toward the garden.

"Look, we can go inside." Fusako's eyes were sparkling like a child's.

With a furtive eye on the lighted window in the watchman's shack, they stole into the dense, man-made forest; there was scarcely room to step. They clasped hands and made their way through the shoulder-high thicket, pushing thorny rose stems aside and stepping over flowers at their feet until they emerged in a corner of the garden occupied by tropical trees and plants, a lush tangle of orchids and banana trees, rubber trees and all varieties of palm.

Seeing Fusako here in her white suit, Ryuji felt that their first meeting must have been in some tropical jungle. Deliberately, cautious of pointed leaves at eye level, they moved together and embraced. The fragrance of her perfume rose above the low droning of mosquitoes: Ryuji was anguished, unaware of time and place.

Outside, only a slender wire fence away, small neon lights were twinkling like goldfish; every few minutes the headlights of a passing car mowed down the shadows of their forest. The glow of a red neon sign flashing across the street carried to Fusako's palm-shadowed face, brought a delicate blush to her white cheeks and blackened her red lips. Ryuji kissed her.

The long kiss plunged them into private pools of sensation. Fusako was aware only of the next day's parting. Stroking Ryuji's cheek, touching the hot, lacquered surfaces where he had shaved, smelling the odor of flesh rising from his agitated chest, she sensed every nerve in his body screaming goodbye. His tight, furious embrace told her how desperately he wanted to affirm that she was real and really with him.

For Ryuji the kiss was death, the very death in love he always dreamed of. The softness of her lips, her mouth so crimson in the darkness he could see it with closed eyes, so infinitely moist, a tepid coral sea, her restless tongue quivering like sea grass . . . in the dark rapture of all this was something directly linked to death. He was perfectly aware that he would leave her in a day, yet he was ready to die happily for her sake. Death roused inside him, stirred.

Then the pale tremor of a ship's horn floated in from the direction of Center Pier and settled over the garden. A nebulous mist of sound, it would never have registered on Ryuji's ear if he hadn't been a sailor. *Funny time of night for a freighter to be pulling out—I wonder how they got her loaded so fast.* The thought broke the spell of the kiss; he opened his eyes. And he could feel the horn probing deep inside him, rousing his passion for the Grand Cause. But what was it? Maybe another name for the tropical sun.

Ryuji drew away from Fusako's lips and began

fumbling in his vest pocket. She waited. There was a harsh rustling of paper and he produced a crooked cigarette and placed it between his lips; but Fusako angrily snatched the lighter out of his hand. He leaned toward her. "Don't expect me to give you a light, because I won't." The lighter flared with a metallic click, the flame danced in her unmoving eyes as she held it to a hemp leaf. The withered tassels should have fired quickly but the flame wouldn't catch. Her engrossment, the steadiness of her hand made Ryuji afraid.

Then the little flame lit up her cheek and he saw the string of tears. Fusako put out the lighter when she realized he had noticed. Ryuji embraced her again and, relieved by the assurance of her tears, he began to cry too.

Noboru waited irritably for his mother to come home. At ten o'clock he heard the telephone ring. A minute later the housekeeper came to his room with a message.

"Your mother just called to say she's going to stay the night at a friend's. She'll be back in the morning to change before she goes to the shop; and you're to spend the evening catching up on all that summer homework."

Never before, not as far back as he could remember, had his mother ever stayed out all night. The development itself was no surprise, but he flushed with rage and apprehension. He had been looking forward all day to the peephole: there was no telling what revelations, what miracles it might have disclosed again tonight. He wasn't at all sleepy, on account of the nap he had taken in the afternoon.

The desk was covered with assignments he had to finish before the new semester began; there were only a few days left. But Ryuji was leaving the next day and then his mother would help him again. Or would she just wander around in a daze, too preoccupied to worry about her own son's homework? Not that it made much difference: Japanese and English and art were the only subjects she could handle. She was never much help with social studies, and he knew more about math and science than she did. How could anyone that bad at math run a business? She was probably always at Mr. Shibuya's mercy.

Noboru opened a textbook and skimmed a few pages but he couldn't concentrate. He was too disturbed by the indisputable fact the Ryuji and his mother were not in the house.

He stood up, sat down, and at last began to pace the small room. What could he do to get to sleep? Go into his mother's room and watch the mast lamps in the harbor? The red lamps on some of the ships blinked on and off all night; there might even be a freighter sailing again, and another screaming horn.

Then he heard the door to the next room open.

Maybe his mother had been trying to fool him and had come home with Ryuji after all. He slipped the drawer quietly out of the dresser and lowered it to the floor. He was already dripping wet.

This time there was a knock at his own door! He couldn't let anyone see the drawer sitting in the middle of the floor at this time of night: he scrambled to the door and pushed against it with all his might. The doorknob rattled harshly.

"What's going on in there? Can't I come in?" But it was the housekeeper's voice. "Are you all right? Go ahead and be stubborn then; but you'd better turn those lights out and get to bed—it's almost eleven."

Noboru was still leaning against the door, maintaining obstinate silence, when a key was rammed into the lock and roughly turned! He was aghast. It had never occurred to him that the housekeeper might have a key: he had assumed that his mother had taken all the keys with her when she went out.

Furious, his brow dripping sweat, he wrenched the doorknob with all his strength; the door didn't open. The housekeeper's footsteps faded as she descended the groaning stairs.

Noboru had hoped to take advantage of this one-in-a-thousand chance by sneaking over to the chief's house and waking him with a password whispered outside his window. Now this last, fervent hope was dashed to bits. He despised all mankind. And he wrote a long entry in his diary, not forgetting to set down Ryuji's crimes.

CHARGES AGAINST RYUJI TSUKAZAKI

ONE: *smiling at me in a cowardly, ingratiating way when I met him this noon.*

TWO: *wearing a dripping-wet shirt and explaining that he had taken a shower in the fountain at the park—just like an old bum.*

THREE: *deciding arbitrarily to spend the night out with Mother, thereby placing me in an awfully isolated position.*

But after thinking it over, Noboru erased the third count. It was obviously a contradiction of the first two, which were aesthetic, idealistic, and therefore objective value judgments. The subjective problem in the third charge was only proof of his own immaturity, not to be construed as a crime on Ryuji's part.

Noboru squeezed a mountain of toothpaste onto his toothbrush and belabored his mouth until the gums bled. Staring into the mirror, he watched a pistachio foam swaddle his irregular teeth until only the shiny pointed edges of the boyish cuspids showed: he was despondent. The smell of peppermint made a purity of his rage.

Tearing off his shirt, Noboru put on his pajama tops and looked around the room. As if it were material evidence, the dresser drawer was still on exhibit in the middle of the floor. He lifted it, surprised by a heaviness he hadn't noticed before, and was about to return it to the chest when he changed his mind and put it down again. He slipped into the space in the wall with practiced ease.

The hole had been closed, he thought for one terrifying instant; then, groping with his fingers, he discovered that it was open as before. There simply wasn't enough light on the other side to reveal it at a glance.

Noboru pressed his eye to the peephole. When the door had opened before, he realized, it had been the housekeeper going in to draw all the curtains. Gradually the pupil strained open and he discerned around the brass bedsteads a glimmer of light, a wisp of brightness hardly more than a trace of mold.

The room as a whole, feverish with a vestige of the noon heat, was as black as the inside of a large coffin, everywhere a shade of darkness, and alive with jostling particles of something Noboru had never seen, the blackest thing in all the world.

CHAPTER EIGHT

T H E Y spent the night in a
small old hotel not far from the docks: Fusako was
afraid she might be recognized at one of the large
downtown hotels. She had often passed this drab, two-
story building but had never imagined as she glanced
through the glass doors at the entrance and saw the
dim, outsized lobby, and the scarred front desk, and the
large steamship calendar bedizening one calcimined
wall, that she would be staying here one day.

They slept for a few hours in the early morning,
then separated until sailing time. Fusako went home to
change clothes before going to work, Ryuji returned to
the pier. He had to substitute for the First Mate, who
was going ashore to do some shopping. He would have
been busy in any case because the maintenance of
ropes and other tackle so important in the loading
operation was one of his regular duties.

The *Rakuyo* was due to sail at six; and thanks to four days and nights of perfect weather, loading had proceeded on schedule. The freighter was bound for Santos, her meandering course to be determined by consignors in ports along the way.

Fusako came home at three, changed into a cotton *yukata* so that Ryuji might have a last look at a woman in kimono, and left for the pier with Noboru. Traffic was light: it was just minutes after four when they arrived. A few trucks and a crane were still clustered around one of the concrete sheds, the boom on the *Rakuyo's* foredeck still wobbled between her hatches and the pier. Fusako decided to wait in the air-conditioned car until Ryuji came down to meet them.

But Noboru couldn't sit still. He bolted out of the car and raced up and down the bustling pier, inspecting the barges moored below and exploring unlocked sheds.

Inside the largest, reaching almost to the crisscross of green steel beams at the ceiling, were stacks of new white wooden crates with black metal clasps at the corners and stamping in English on the side slats. Noboru, watching a siding fade to nothing amid the towering freight, felt a thrill of joy at having come to the end of the dream that railroads wake in children, and mild disappointment: it was like tracing the course of a familiar river and discovering its tiny source.

"Mom! Hey, Mom!" Racing back to the car, Noboru

drummed on the window: he had spotted Ryuji standing near the windlass in the ship's prow.

Fusako got out of the car and they waved at the
high distant figure in a dirty khaki shirt. Ryuji raised
one hand in reply, then moved busily out of sight.
Noboru thought of the sailor toiling now, and soon to
sail away; and he was flushed with pride.

Fusako could only wait for Ryuji to appear again.
Unfurling a parasol with a silver handle, she watched
the *Rakuyo*'s swaying hawsers cut thick gashes across
the harbor's face. The dock was broiling under the
western sun, light-washed and overbright; and eating
into all the steel and concrete, like the salt in a sea
wind, was a strong, smarting grief. The same grief was
diffused through the bright air, its force imparting to
the occasional clatter of deck plates and the crash of
hurled cables a long, hollow reverberation.

The concrete pier trapped the heat and hurled it
back as a scorching glare; the light breeze blowing off
the water brought no relief.

They squatted at the edge of the sea wall with their
backs to the ferocious sun, and stared at the wavelets
mincing in to break and foam against the white-flecked
stone. Rocking slightly like a rough-hewn cradle, one of
the barges moored below edged toward the wall, then
slipped back while another sidled in. A sea gull
skimmed over the wash that flapped on the open decks;
a shiny log floating amid other garbage on the dirty

water rode around and around on the eddying swell.
The waves advanced in tiers, flank blending subtly with
azure flank until it seemed that this endlessly repeated
pattern was all they could see as they gazed at the
water.

Noboru read off the draft numbers painted on the
Rakuyo's side; 60 was just above the water, 84 and 86
bracketed the water line, 90 was almost as high as the
haweshole.

"Do you think the water ever gets that high? Boy, it
must be really something if it does."

Noboru had guessed his mother's mood and she was
reminding him as she stared out to sea of that lonely,
naked figure in front of the mirror: the question was as
boyish as he could make it, but Fusako didn't answer.

Across the harbor basin, pale gray smoke hovered
above the streets of Naka Ward; the red-and-white-
striped beacon tower aspired to clearer sky. The offing
was a dense forest of white masts and, still farther out,
a bank of clouds luminous in the late afternoon sunlight
heaped and twisted above the water.

A steam launch towing an unloaded barge pulled
away from the far side of the *Rakuyo* and chugged out
of sight.

It was just after five when Ryuji came off the ship.
The silver chains which would raise the gangplank had
already been attached. A gang of longshoremen wearing yellow helmets had filed down the gangplank, piled

into a Longshoremen's Union bus, and left the pier. The eight-ton Port Authority derrick had gone, the hatches had been bolted down. Then, finally, Ryuji appeared.

Noboru and Fusako chased long shadows toward the sailor. Ryuji squashed Noboru's straw hat with the palm of his hand and laughed as the boy struggled to pull the brim up over his eyes. The work had exhilarated him.

"We'll be leaving any minute now. I'll be aft when we cast off." Ryuji gestured toward the distant stern.

"I decided to wear a kimono. You won't be seeing any for quite a while now—"

"I guess not—except maybe on old nisei ladies traveling with American tours."

They found surprisingly little to say. Fusako considered mentioning how lonely she was going to be and decided not to. The parting, like the white fruit of an apple discoloring instantly around the bite, had begun three days before when they had met aboard the *Rakuyo*. Saying goodbye now entailed not a single new emotion.

Noboru, as he affected childishness, was standing guard over the perfection of the adults, the moment. His was the sentinel's role. The less time they had, the better. The shorter this meeting was, the less perfection would be marred. For the moment, as a man leaving a woman behind to voyage around the world, as a sailor, and as a Second Mate, Ryuji was perfect. So was his mother. As a woman to be left behind, as a beautiful sailcloth full-blown with happy memories and the grief of parting, she was perfect too. Both had blundered dangerously during the past two days but at the moment their behavior was beyond reproach. If only Ryuji didn't say something ridiculous and spoil it all before he was safely under way. Peering from beneath the broad brim of his straw hat, Noboru anxiously studied first one face and then the other.

Ryuji wanted to kiss Fusako but he was intimidated by Noboru. Besides, like a man who knows he is dying, he felt a need to be equally tender to all. At the moment, the memories and feelings of others seemed far more important than his own; yet somewhere beneath the sweet agony of self-denial was a desire to get away as quickly as possible.

Fusako still couldn't permit herself to imagine the anxious, exhausting wait to come. She devoured the man with her eyes, testing the sufficiency of that bond. But how self-contained he looked, like a refractory object not even attempting to extend itself beyond its contours. She wished he could be something less defined, like mist. This horrid hulk was too much like rock to fade from memory: the heavy brows, for example, or the too solid shoulders. . . .

"Don't forget to write—and use all different kinds of

stamps," Norboru said, perfectly in command of his
role.

"You bet. I'll send something from every port. And
you write too. A sailor looks forward to letters more
than anything."

He explained that he had to go aboard to help with
the final preparations. They all shook hands. Ryuji
climbed the silvery gangplank, turned at the top, and
waved his cap.

The sun was just above the warehouse roofs, setting
fire to the western sky and searing shadow images of
king posts and mushroom ventilators into the dazzling
white steel of the bridge. Noboru watched the sea gulls
wheeling overhead; their wings were dark, their bellies,
when they breasted the light, turned yellow as yokes.

Trucks and cranes and dollies had withdrawn from
the *Rakuyo* and the dock was empty and still, awash in
light. A deckhand dwarfed by distance was still scrub-
bing a high railing on the *Rakuyo*'s deck and another, a
patch over one eye and a paint can in his hand, painting what might have been a window frame. Noboru
hadn't noticed the blue and white and red signal flags
being hoisted up the mast; at the top of the spire, the
blue peter fluttered. They walked slowly toward the
stern.

All the louvered, dark-green warehouse doors were
lowered; large "No Smoking" signs and the names of

major ports scrawled in chalk—Singapore, Hong Kong, Lagos—covered the dismal reach of wall. Tires and trash cans and the dollies parked in neat rows cast their long shadows across the concrete pier.

The stern high above them was still deserted. There was a quiet sound of water draining, a Japanese flag flapped in the shadow of the anchor davit.

The first stridulous blast of the horn came at fifteen minutes to six. Noboru, listening, knew that the phantom he had watched two nights before was real, understood that he was present at the spot where all dreams began and ended. Then he saw Ryuji; he was standing next to the Japanese flag.

"He might hear you if you yell loud enough," Fusako urged. The shout left his throat just as the horn subsided: he was horrified by the shrillness of his voice. Ryuji peered down at them and waved; he was too far away to see the expression on his face. Then he turned back to his work with the same twist of his shoulders that had faced him toward the moonlit horn, and didn't look their way again.

Fusako glanced toward the prow. The gangplank had been raised; the last link between ship and shore was broken. The *Rakuyo*'s green-and-cream-colored side looked like the blade of a colossal ax fallen out of the heavens to cleave the shore asunder.

Smoke began to pour from the smokestacks. Utterly

black, it billowed into the sky in huge clouds which rose to smudge the pale zenith.

"Stand by, fore-station—make ready to weigh anchor."

"Take up on that slack!" There was another short blast on the horn.

"That's good, fore-station."

"Right."

"Weigh anchor—head line away—shore lines away!"

The *Rakuyo* inched away from the pier as the tugboat toiled into the harbor with the stern in tow. The breadth of water sparkling between the ship and the sea wall fanned open, and even as their eyes were pursuing the receding glitter of the gold braid on Ryuji's cap, the ship had pivoted a full ninety degrees and was perpendicular to the pier.

The *Rakuyo* was transformed into an illusory phantom as angles altered from one instant to the next. Gradually, as the stern was towed farther out into the harbor, the long ship folded like a paneled screen while the superstructure on deck overlapped, piled into impacted tiers, and, trapping sunlight in every pocket and dent, soared skyward like a shining pagoda of steel. But the effect was only momentary. Now the tug began to circle back in order to face the prow toward open sea, and the storied tower thrusting up from the deck was dismantled; each object in order from prow to stern resumed its proper shape until finally the stern itself reappeared and a matchstick figure just recognizable as Ryuji swung back into the splendor of the setting sun.

"Tow lines away—" The voice on the loudspeaker was still clear when it reached them on the wind. The tug pulled away.

Poising motionless on the water, the ship sounded three blasts on her horn. Uneasy silence followed, an interval of quiescence during which it seemed that Ryuji aboard ship and Fusako and Noboru on the pier were trapped in the same viscous moment of time.

Finally, rocking the whole harbor and carrying to every city window; besetting kitchens with dinner on the stove, and shoddy hotel bedrooms where sheets are never changed, and desks waiting for children to come home, and schools and tennis courts and graveyards; plunging everything into a moment of grief and ruthlessly tearing even the hearts of the uninvolved, the *Rakuyo*'s horn screamed one last enormous farewell. Trailing white smoke, she sailed straight out to sea. Ryuji was lost from sight.

PART TWO

WINTER

CHAPTER ONE

AT nine o'clock in the morning on December 30, Ryuji emerged from the customs shed at Center Pier. Fusako was there to meet him.

Center Pier was a curious abstraction of a neighborhood. The streets were unpeopled and too clean; the plane trees lining them were withered. Down a siding which ran between archaic red-brick warehouses and a pseudo-Renaissance shipping office chugged an ancient steam engine huffing clouds of black smoke. Even the little railroad crossing seemed unauthentic, as though it belonged with a set of toy trains. The sea was responsible for the unreality of the place, for it was to her service alone that the streets, the buildings, even the dumb bricks in the wall were pledged. The sea had simplified and abstracted, and the pier in turn had lost its sense of reality and appeared to be dwelling within a dream.

Besides, it was raining. Rich cinnabar gushed out of the old brick walls and washed into puddles on the street. The masts spiring above the roofs were dripping wet.

Not wanting to attract attention, Fusako waited in the back seat of the car. Through the rain-streaked window she watched the crew emerge one by one from the weather-beaten wooden shed. Ryuji paused for a minute in the doorway to turn up the collar of his pea coat and pull his cap low over his eyes. Then he hunched into the rain, carrying an old zippered bag. Fusako sent her chauffeur running out to call him.

He came hurtling into the car like a piece of bulky, rain-soaked baggage. "I knew you'd come—I knew it," he gasped, seizing the shoulders of Fusako's mink coat.

His cheeks were streaked with rain—or were those tears?—and he was more sunburned than before. Fusako had paled: her white face was like a window opened in the dim interior of the car. They kissed, and they were crying. Ryuji slipped his hands under Fusako's coat and clutched wildly at her body as though searching for life in a corpse he had saved from drowning, locked his arms around her supple waist and replenished his heart and mind with the details of her. It was only a six- or seven-minute ride to the house. Finally, as the car was crossing Yamashita Bridge, they were able to begin a normal conversation.

"Thanks for all the letters. I read every one a hundred times."

"I did yours too. You can stay with us at least through New Year's, can't you?"

"Thanks. . . . How's Noboru been?"

"He wanted to come and meet you at the pier but he caught a little cold and had to go to bed. Oh, it's nothing serious—hardly any fever—"

The conversation was ordinary, remarks any landsmen might exchange, and it came easily. They had imagined during the months apart that their conversation would be difficult when they met again; restoring the bond between them to what it had been after three summer days had seemed impossible. Why should things proceed as smoothly as an arm slips into the sleeve of a coat unworn for half a year?

But the tears of joy had washed anxiety away and lifted them to a height where nothing was impossible. Ryuji was as if paralyzed: the sight of familiar places, places they had visited together, failed to move him. That Yamashita Park and Marine Tower should now appear just as he had often pictured them seemed only obvious, inevitable. And the smoking drizzle of rain, by softening the too distinct scenery and making of it something closer to the images in memory, only heightened the reality of it all. Ryuji expected for some time after he disembarked to feel the world tottering precariously beneath his feet, and yet today more than ever before, like a piece in a jigsaw puzzle, he felt snugly in place in an anchored, amiable world.

They turned right off the bridge, drove for a short time along the canal, buried under gray tarpaulined barges, and began climbing the hill past the French Consulate. High in the sky, disheveled clouds brightened and churned apart; the rain was letting up. They were at the top of the hill now, passing the entrance to the park. The car turned left into a lane and stopped in front of the Kuroda house. From the gate to the front door was only a few steps, but the tile walk was soaking wet. The old chauffeur held an umbrella over Fusako as he escorted her to the door and then rang the bell.

When the housekeeper appeared, Fusako told her to turn on the light in the vestibule. Ryuji stepped over the low sill and entered the dimness.

In the instant needed to cross the threshold, a subtle doubt assailed him. Presumably, the glittering ring they had re-entered together was just as they had left it. The difference was ineffably slight, but something, somewhere, had changed. Fusako had been careful never to allude to the future, neither when they had said goodbye at the end of the summer nor in any of her many letters, yet their embrace a few minutes before had made clear that it was here to this house, together, that both were longing to return. But Ryuji's eagerness wouldn't permit him to pause and consider the discrepancy further. He didn't even notice that he was entering an altogether different house.

"It's been just pouring," Fusako was saying. "It seems to be letting up a little now, though." Then the light in the vestibule clicked on and the imported marble floor floated into view.

A fire was blazing in the living-room fireplace, and installed on the mantel in readiness for New Year's Day was a small wooden stand laden with oblatory rice-cakes and garlanded in the traditional manner with whitebeam and kelp and bunches of sea grapes. The housekeeper brought them some tea and managed a creditable greeting: "It's very nice to see you back again. Noboru and Mrs. Kuroda have been excited all week."

The only changes in the living room were some new samples of Fusako's embroidery and a small tennis trophy on display in one corner. She guided Ryuji around the room, explaining each addition as she came to it. The moment he had sailed, her zeal for tennis and embroidery had increased. She had been playing at the club near the Myokoji Temple every weekend, sometimes even stealing away from the shop on weekday afternoons; the evenings she had spent alone in her room, embroidering on silk. Many of her recent patterns had something to do with ships. The new cushions, completed during the autumn, were decorated with old-fashioned wheels and small stylized fleets of Portuguese schooners. The trophy was for women's doubles; she had won it in the club's end-of-the-year tournament. For Ryuji, all this was proof of her chastity during his absence.

"But nothing really wonderful happened," Fusako said. "Not while you were away. . . ."

She confessed how peeved she had been to discover herself waiting for him despite her determination not to. She had thrown herself into her work confident that he was forgotten, and when the last customer for the day had left and the shop was hushed, she would hear the fountain bubbling in the patio. And listening, be struck with terror. Then she knew that she was waiting. . . .

This time, Fusako was able to express herself with fluency and candor. The bold letters she had been writing week after week had granted her an unexpected new freedom. And Ryuji was more talkative than before, more animated. The change began one day in Honolulu when he received Fusako's first letter. He became noticeably more friendly, even began to enjoy the gab sessions in the mess room. It wasn't long after that before the *Rakuyo*'s officers knew all the details of his love.

"Do you feel like going up and saying hello to

Noboru? He was so excited about seeing you, I'll bet he
didn't get a decent night's sleep either."

Ryuji rose from his chair. It was clear now, beyond
a doubt: he was the man they had been waiting for, the
man they loved.

Taking a present for Noboru out of his suitcase,
Ryuji followed Fusako up the same dark stairs he had
climbed on trembling tiptoe that summer night. This
time, his steps were the resolute tread of a man who has
been included.

In bed upstairs, Noboru listened to the ascending
footsteps. He was tense from waiting, his body under
the covers stiff as a board, and yet, somehow, these
weren't quite the footsteps he had expected.

There was a knock on his door and it swung open.
Noboru saw a reddish-brown baby crocodile.

The beast hovered in the doorway, floating in the
watery light which was pouring into the room from the
sky outside, clear now and bright, and for an instant
the glittering glass-bead eyes, and the gaping mouth,
and the stiffened legs paddling the air, seemed to come
alive. A question struggled through the muddle of his
slightly feverish mind: has anyone ever used something
alive for a coat of arms? Once Ryuji had told him about
the Coral Sea: the water inside an atoll was as still as
the surface of a pond, but in the offing, huge waves
thundered to pieces against the outer reef and the

crashing crests of white foam looked like hugely distant phantoms. His headache, which, compared with yesterday's, had receded into the distance, was like a white crest billowing beyond the atoll. And the crocodile was the headache's coat of arms, the symbol of his own distant authority. It was true that sickness had touched the boy's face with majesty.

"Like him? He's for you." Ryuji had been standing just outside the door, holding the crocodile at arm's length. Now he stepped into the room. He was wearing a gray turtleneck sweater; his face was deeply tanned.

Noboru had prepared for Ryuji's entrance by resolving not to smile with pleasure. Using illness as a pretext, he succeeded in maintaining a glum face.

"That's strange! He was so happy and excited just a little while ago. Do you feel feverish again, dear?" An unwarranted little speech! Never before had his mother seemed such a petty person.

"A story goes with this," Ryuji went on, unmindful of the tension in the room. He placed the beast next to Noboru's pillow. "This crocodile was stuffed by the Indians in Brazil. Those tribesmen are authentic Indians. And when carnival time comes around, the warriors put crocodiles like this one or sometimes stuffed water fowl on their heads, in front of the feathers they wear in their hair. And they strap three little round mirrors to their foreheads. When those mirrors catch the light from the bonfires, they look just like . . . three-eyed devils. They string leopard teeth around their throats, and wrap themselves in leopard skins. And they all have quivers on their backs, and beautiful bows, and different-colored arrows. Anyway, that's the story on this crocodile. It's part of the ceremonial dress the Brazilian Indians wear at carnival time."

"Thanks," Noboru said. He ran his hand over the glossy bumps on the crocodile's back and stroked the shriveled limbs. Then he inspected the dust which had accumulated beneath the red glass-bead eyes while the beast had crouched on a shelf in some Brazilian country store, and thought about what Ryuji had said. The room was too hot; the sheets were feverish, wrinkled, damp. The bits of skin on the pillow had flaked off Noboru's dried lips. He had been picking at them furtively a few minutes before. Just as he began to worry that his lips might look too red, he glanced involuntarily toward the drawer that concealed the peephole. Now he had done it! He was in agony. What if the adults traced his gaze and leveled suspicious eyes on the wall? But no, it was all right. They were even more insensible than he had suspected: they were cradled in the numbing arms of love.

Noboru stared hard at the sailor. His sun-blackened face looked even more virile than before, the thick eyebrows and white teeth more sharply accented. But Noboru had sensed something unnatural about the sailor's monologue, a forced attempt to relate to his own fancies, a truckling to the exaggerated sentiments he had set down in his frequent letters. There was something counterfeit about this Ryuji. When he couldn't bear it any longer, Noboru spoke. "I don't know—there's something phony about this . . ."

"Are you kidding? Because he's so small?" It was a good-natured misunderstanding. "Even crocodiles are small when they're kids. Try going to the zoo sometime."

"Noboru! I'm surprised at you. Now why don't you stop being so impolite and show Mr. Tsukazaki your stamp album."

But before he could move a hand, his mother had snatched the album from the desk and was showing Ryuji the carefully mounted stamps he had mailed to Noboru from ports around the world.

She sat in the chair with her face toward the light and turned the pages while Ryuji, one arm across the chair, looked over her shoulder. Noboru noticed they both had handsome profiles: the thin, clear winter light silvered the bridges of their noses. They seemed oblivious of his presence in the room.

"Mr. Tsukazaki, when will you be sailing again?" Noboru asked abruptly.

His mother turned to him with a shocked face and he could see that she had paled. It was the question she most wanted to ask, and most dreaded. Ryuji was posing near the window with his back to them. He half closed his eyes, and then, very slowly, said: "I'm not sure yet."

Noboru was stunned. Fusako didn't speak, but she looked like a bottle full of feeling boiling against the small cork stopper. Her expression might have meant joy or sorrow—a woman's sodden face. To Noboru, she looked like a washerwoman.

A brief pause, and Ryuji calmly spoke again. His tone was sympathetic, the compassion a man feels when he is certain he holds the power to affect another's fate: "At any rate, it'll take at least until after New Year's to get the ship unloaded. . . ."

Red with rage and coughing violently, Noboru pulled his diary from under the pillow as soon as they had left, and wrote a short entry.

CHARGES AGAINST RYUJI TSUKAZAKI
THREE: *answering, when I asked when he would be sailing again: "I'm not sure yet."*

Noboru put down his pen and thought for a minute while his anger mounted. Then he added:

FOUR: *coming back here again in the first place.*

But soon he began to feel ashamed of his anger. What good had been all that training in "absolute dispassion"? He carefully explored every corner of his heart to make certain not even a fragment of rage remained, and then reread what he had written. When he had finished, he was convinced: revision would not be necessary.

Then he heard a stirring in the next room. Apparently his mother had gone into the bedroom. Ryuji seemed to be there too . . . the door to his own room wasn't locked. Noboru's heart began to hammer. How, he wondered, in an unlocked room at this time of morning and quickly—that was important—could he remove the drawer and steal into the space in the wall without being discovered?

CHAPTER TWO

F usako's present was an armadillo pocketbook. It was a bizarre affair, with a handle that looked like a rat's neck, and crude clasps and stitching, but she left the house with it happily and displayed it proudly at the shop while Mr. Shibuya scowled his disapproval.

They spent the last day of the year apart: Fusako was needed at Rex and Ryuji had to take the afternoon watch. This time it seemed perfectly natural that they should go separate ways for half a day.

It was after ten when Fusako returned that evening. Ryuji had been helping Noboru and the housekeeper with the traditional New Year's Eve cleaning and together they had managed to finish the job more quickly than in previous years. Ryuji issued brisk instructions as though he were directing a scrub-down on the deck, and Noboru, whose fever had come down that morning, carried out his orders with delight.

Fusako came in as they were descending the stairs with mops and pails after having cleaned all the upstairs rooms. Ryuji had rolled up the sleeves of his sweater and bound a towel around his head; Noboru was turbaned in the same fashion, his cheeks flushed and glowing. The scene surprised and delighted Fusako, but she couldn't help worrying a little about Noboru's health.

"Stop worrying so much! Working up a good sweat's the best way to kick a cold." The remark may have been crude as an attempt at reassurance but at least it was "man talk," something Fusako's house hadn't heard for a long time. The walls and the old beams in the ceiling seemed to shrink from the masculine utterance.

When the whole family had gathered to listen to the midnight bells and feast on special buckwheat noodles, the housekeeper told an anecdote from her past which she repeated every New Year's Eve: "At the Macgregors'—that's the folks I used to work for—New Year's Eve always meant a big party with lots of company. And at twelve o'clock on the dot everybody started kissing everybody else like it wasn't anything! One time I even had an old Irish gentleman with whiskers smooch me on the cheek—he just hung on there like he was a leech or something. . . ."

Ryuji embraced Fusako as soon as they were alone in the bedroom. Later, when the first pale promise of the dawn appeared, he proposed something childish: why didn't they walk over to the park and watch the first sunrise of the New Year? Fusako was captivated by the lunacy of racing into the cold. She jumped out of bed and bundled into everything she could get on— tights, slacks, a cashmere sweater, and a gorgeous Danish ski sweater over that; and tiptoeing down the stairs, they unlocked the front door and stepped outside.

The dawn air felt good against their heated bodies. Racing into the deserted park, they laughed out loud and chased each other in and out among the fir trees, and took deep breaths, vying to see who could exhale the whitest steam into the cold, dark air. They felt as though thin crusts of ice were coating their love-staled mouths.

It was well past six when they leaned against the railing that overlooked the harbor: Venus had banked into the south. Though the lights of buildings and the red lamps blinking on distant masts were still bright, and though the beacon's red and green blades of light still knifed through the darkness in the park, outlines of houses could be discerned and the sky was touched with reddish purple.

Small and distant, the first cock call of the year reached them on the chill morning wind, a tragic, fitful cry. "May this be a good year for us all." Fusako spoke her prayer aloud. It was cold, and when she nestled her cheek against Ryuji's he kissed the lips so close to his and said: "It will be. It has to be."

Gradually a blurred form at the water's edge was sharpening into a building. As Ryuji stared at a red bulb blooming above an emergency exit, he became painfully conscious of the texture of shore life. He would be thirty-four in May. It was time to abandon the dream he had cherished too long. Time to realize that no specially tailored glory was waiting for him. Time, no matter if the feeble eaves lamps still defied the green-gray light of morning by refusing to come awake, to open his eyes.

Though it was New Year's Day, a submerged tremolo pervaded the harbor. Every few minutes a barge unraveled from the moored fleet and hacked dryly down the canal. As a rosy hue stained the surface of the water and seemed to inflate itself into round abundance, the poles of light slanting away from anchored ships began to dwindle. Twenty minutes past six: the mercury lamps in the park clicked out.

"Are you getting cold?" Ryuji asked.

"My gums are stinging, it's so cold—but I don't mind. The sun will be coming up any minute now."

Are you getting cold? . . . Are you getting cold? Ryuji asked again and again, and all the time he was directing another question to himself: Are you really going to give it up? *The feeling of the sea, the dark, drunken feeling that unearthly rolling always brings?*

*The thrill of saying goodbye? The sweet tears you weep
for your song? Are you going to give up the life which
has detached you from the world, kept you remote, im-
pelled you toward the pinnacle of manliness?* The
secret yearning for death. The glory beyond and
the death beyond. Everything was "beyond," wrong or
right, had always been "beyond." *Are you going to give
that up?* His heart in spasm because he was always in
contact with the ocean's dark swell and the lofty light
from the edge of the clouds, twisting, withering until it
clogged and then swelling up again, and he unable to
distinguish the most exalted feelings from the meanest
and that not mattering really since he could hold the
sea responsible—*are you going to give up that luminous freedom?*

And yet Ryuji had discovered on the return leg of
his last voyage that he was tired, tired to death of the
squalor and the boredom in a sailor's life. He was convinced that he had tasted it all, even the lees, and he
was glutted. What a fool he'd been! There was no glory
to be found, not anywhere in the world. Not in the
Northern Hemisphere. Not in the Southern Hemisphere. Not even beneath that star every sailor dreams
about, the Southern Cross!

Now they could make out the lumber yards beyond
the canal: roosters had crowed at the sky until a coy
blush spread across her face. Finally the mast lamps
blinked out and ships withdrew like phantoms into the

fog that shrouded the harbor. Then, as an angry red began to smolder along the edges of the sky, the space of park behind them unfurled into whitish emptiness and the skirts on the beacon beam fell away, leaving only glinting needlepoints of red and green light.

It was very cold; leaning against the railing with their arms around each other, they stamped their feet.

"It can't be long now," Fusako said, her voice rising above the chatter of small birds. The lipstick she had dashed on before they left the house, a spot of vivid red rising out of the whiteness of her chilled, drawn face, looked beautiful to Ryuji.

A minute later, far to the right of the floating lumber and surprisingly high up, a gauzy red ring loomed in the slate-gray sky. Immediately the sun became a globe of pure red but still so weak they could look straight at it, a blood-red moon.

"I know this will be a good year; it couldn't be anything else with us here like this, watching the first sunrise together. And you know something? This is the first time I've ever seen the sunrise on New Year's Day." Fusako's voice warped in the cold. Ryuji heard himself bellow in the resolute voice he used to shout orders into the wind on the winter deck: "Will you marry me?"

"What?"

Annoyed at having to repeat himself, he blurted things better left unsaid: "I'm asking you to marry me.

I may be just a dumb sailor but I've never done anything I'm ashamed of. You may laugh when I say this,
but I have nearly two million yen saved up—you can
see my bankbook later. That's everything I have to my
name and I'm going to give it all to you whether you
marry me or not."

His artless proposal touched the worldly lady more
deeply than he knew. Overjoyed, Fusako began to
cry.

The sun was blazing now, too dazzlingly bright for
Ryuji's anxious eyes, and the whistle-wailing, gear-
grinding cacophony of the harbor was surging toward
full pitch. The horizon was misted over, the sun's reflection spreading like a reddish haze over the surface of
the water.

"Yes—of course I will. But I think there are some
problems we ought to discuss first. There's Noboru, for
example, and my work at the shop. Can I make just one
condition? What you've just said, I mean—if you're
planning to leave again soon—it would be hard. . . ."

"I won't be sailing again for a while. As a matter of
fact . . ." Ryuji faltered, and was silent.

There wasn't a single Japanese room in Fusako's
house; her mode of living was thoroughly Western except on New Year's Day, when she observed tradition
by serving the special New Year's breakfast on lacquered trays and drinking toasts with spiced sake.

Ryuji hadn't slept at all. He washed his face with "young water," the first water drawn in the year, and went into the dining room. It was a strange feeling, as though he were still in Europe, at the Japanese Consulate in some northern seaport. In the past, he and the other officers of the *Rakuyo* had been invited to New Year's breakfast at consulates abroad: the sake dipper and the wooden cups stacked on a stand inlaid with gold, and the lacquered boxes filled with traditional side dishes, were always arrayed on a table in a bright Western dining room just as they were here.

Noboru came down wearing a new necktie, and New Year's congratulations were exchanged. In previous years Noboru had always drunk the first toast, but when the time came and he reached for the uppermost and smallest of the three cups, Fusako stopped him with a reproving look.

Pretending to be embarrassed, he simpered:

"It seems pretty silly for Mr. Tsukazaki to drink out of the smallest." But his eyes never left the cup. It seemed to wither in the grasp of the huge, calloused hand that carried it to the sailor's lips. Buried under the thick fingers of a hand accustomed to grappling rope, the vermilion plum-branch cup looked horribly vulgar.

When he had finished the toast, Ryuji began an account of a hurricane in the Caribbean before Noboru even had a chance to coax him:

"When the pitching gets really bad you can hardly

cook your rice. But you manage somehow and then eat it plain, just squeezed into little balls. Of course, the bowls won't stay put on a table, so you push the desks in the lounge up against the wall and sit on the floor and try to gulp it down.

"But this hurricane in the Caribbean was really something. The *Rakuyo* was built overseas more than twenty years ago and she starts leaking when you hit rough weather. Well, this time the water came pouring in around the rivet holes in the hull. And at a time like that there's no difference between officers and deckhands, everybody works together like drowning rats, bailing and throwing mats down and pouring cement as fast as you can get it mixed. And even if you get slammed against a wall or hurled into the dark when the power shorts out, you haven't got time to be scared.

"I'll tell you one thing, though: no matter how long you've been on a ship, you never get used to storms. I mean you're sure every time you run into one that your number is up. Anyway, the day before this last hurricane the sunset looked too much like a big fire and the red in the sky was kind of murky and the water was quiet as a lake. I had sort of a feeling then that something was coming—"

"Stop it, please stop!" Fusako screamed, clapping her hands over her ears. "Please don't talk about things like that any more."

His mother's histrionics annoyed Noboru: why did

she have to cover her ears and protest about an adventure story which obviously was being told for his benefit! Or had it been intended for her in the first place?

The thought made him uncomfortable. Ryuji had told the same sort of sea story before, but this time his delivery seemed different. The tone of his voice reminded Noboru of a peddler selling sundry wares while he handled them with dirty hands. Unsling a pack from your back and spread it open on the ground for all to see: one hurricane Caribbean-style—scenery along the banks of the Panama Canal—a carnival smeared in red dust from the Brazilian countryside—a tropical rainstorm flooding a village in the twinkling of an eye—bright parrots hollering beneath a dark sky. . . . No doubt about it: Ryuji did have a pack of wares.

CHAPTER THREE

O N the fifth of January the *Rakuyo* sailed and Ryuji was not aboard. He stayed on as a guest in the Kuroda house.

Rex opened on the sixth. Relieved and in high spirits because Ryuji had stayed behind, Fusako arrived at the shop just before noon and received New Year's congratulations from Mr. Shibuya and the rest of the staff. Waiting on her desk was an invoice from an English distributor:

Messrs. Rex, Ltd., Yokohama

ORDER NO. 1062-B

The shipment had arrived during the vacation on the *El Dorado;* there were two and a half dozen men's vests and pullovers, and a dozen and a half pairs of sports slacks, sizes 34, 38, and 40. Including the 10 per cent commission for the distributor, the bill came to ninety thousand yen. Even if they shelved the order for a month or so they could count on clearing fifty thousand yet in profits: half the merchandise was on special order and could be sold at any time. And not having to worry about depreciation no matter how long the rest remained on the shelf was the advantage of handling English products through a first-rate distributor. The retail prices were established in England and their account would be canceled if they tried to undersell.

Mr. Shibuya came into the office and announced: "The Jackson Company is having a pre-season showing of their spring and summer collections on the twenty-fifth. We have received an invitation."

"Oh? I suppose that means we'll be competing with buyers from the big Tokyo stores again—not that those people aren't all blind as bats."

"They have no feel for fabric or design because they have never worn fine clothes themselves."

"Isn't it the truth!" Fusako noted the date in the memo book on her desk. "Is it tomorrow that we're supposed to go to the Foreign Trade Ministry? Bureaucrats always make me so nervous, I'll probably just sit there and grin. I'm counting on you to get us through."

"I'll do what I can. One of the senior clerks happens to be an old friend."

"Oh yes, you've mentioned that before—I feel better already."

Hoping to satisfy the tastes of some new customers, Rex had entered into a special agreement with the Men's Town and Country Shop in New York: letters of credit had already been issued and now it was up to Fusako to apply through the Foreign Trade Ministry for an import license.

"I've been meaning to ask," Fusako said abruptly, her eyes on the V neck of the thin old dandy's camel's-hair vest, "how you've been feeling lately."

"Not awfully well, thank you. I imagine it's my arthritis acting up again, but the pain seems to be spreading."

"Well, have you been to see a doctor?"

"No, what with the holiday rush and everything . . ."

"But you haven't been feeling well since before New Year's."

"I don't have time to waste sitting around in a doctor's office, especially this time of year."

"I still wish you'd have someone look at you right away. If anything happened to you, we'd be out of business."

The old man smiled vaguely, one wrinkled white hand fussing nervously with the tight knot in his necktie.

A salesgirl came in to say that Miss Yoriko Kasuga had arrived.

Fusako went down to the patio. This time Yoriko had come alone. She was wearing a mink coat, peering into a showcase with her back turned. When she had decided on some Lancôme lipstick and a Pelican fountain pen, Fusako invited her to lunch: the famous actress beamed with pleasure. Fusako took her to Le

Centaure, a small French restaurant near the harbor where yachtsmen often gathered. The proprietor was an old gourmet who once had worked at the French Consulate.

Fusako looked at the actress as though to measure the loneliness of this simple, somehow stolid woman. Yoriko had received not one of the awards she had been counting on for the past year, and obviously her excursion to Yokohama today was an escape from the eyes society levels on a star who has failed to win an award. Though she must have had followers beyond counting, the only person with whom she could be frank and at ease was the proprietress of a Yokohama luxury shop, not even a close friend.

Fusako decided it would be best not to mention movie awards during lunch.

They drank a bottle of the restaurant's celebrated *vin de maison* with their bouillabaisse. Fusako had to order for Yoriko because she couldn't read the French menu.

"You know, Mama, you're really beautiful," the large beauty said abruptly. "I'd give anything to look like you." Yoriko slighted her own beauty more than any woman Fusako knew. The actress had marvelous breasts, gorgeous eyes, a fine-sculptured nose, and voluptuous lips, and yet she was tormented by vague feelings of inferiority. She even believed, and it pained her not a little, that the awards committee had passed

her by because men watching her on the screen saw
only a woman they would love to take to bed.

Fusako watched the famous, beautiful, unhappy
woman flush with contentment as she decorated her
name in an autograph book produced by the waitress.
Yoriko's reaction to an autograph book was always a
good indication of her mood. And judging from the
drunken generosity with which she was flourishing her
pen just now, a fan would need only to ask for one of
her breasts to receive it.

"The only people in this world I really trust are my
fans—even if they do forget you so fast," Yoriko mum-
bled as she lit an imported woman's cigarette.

"Don't you trust me?" Fusako teased. She could
predict Yoriko's felicitous response to such a question.

"Do you think I'd come all the way to Yokohama if I
didn't? You're the only real friend I have. Honestly, you
are. I haven't felt this relaxed in ages and it's all thanks
to you, Mama." That name again! Fusako winced.

The walls of the restaurant were decorated with
water-color paintings of famous yachts, bright red
checkered tablecloths covered the empty tables; they
were the only people in the small room. The old window frames began to creak in the wind and a page of a
newspaper scudded down the empty street. The window opened on a dismal reach of ashen warehouse walls.

Yoriko kept her mink coat draped around her
shoulders while she ate: an imposing necklace of heavy

gold chain swayed on her stately chest. She had es-
caped the scandal-loving world, she had even eluded
her own ambition, and now, like a muscular woman
laborer lazing in the sun between wearisome tasks, she
was content. Though her reasons for sorrow or joy
rarely seemed convincing to the observer, Yoriko managed to support a family of ten, and it was at moments
like this that the source of her vitality became apparent. She derived her strength from something she herself was least aware of: her beauty.

Fusako had a sudden feeling that she would find in
Yoriko the ideal confidante. Thereupon she began to tell
about Ryuji, and the happiness in the story made her so
drunk that she revealed every intimate detail.

"Is that right! And did he really give you his seal
and a bankbook with two million yen on deposit?"

"I tried to refuse, but he wouldn't take no for an
answer."

"But there was no reason for you to have refused.
And wasn't that a manly thing to do! Of course, the
money is only pennies as far as you're concerned, but
it's the spirit behind it that counts. I would never have
dreamed that there were men like that around any-
more. Especially since the only men who come near
me are freeloaders out for whatever they can get. I
hope you realize how lucky you are."

Fusako had never dreamed that Yoriko could be
practical and she was astonished when, having listened

to the whole story, the actress promptly prescribed a course of action.

A prerequisite of any marriage, she began, was an investigation by a private detective agency. Fusako would need a photograph of Ryuji and about thirty thousand yen. If she hurried them she could have the results within a week. Yoriko would be happy to recommend a reliable agency.

Though she didn't imagine there was any cause for worry in this case, there was always the possibility that a sailor might have an ugly disease: it would be best if they exchanged health certificates, Ryuji accompanying Fusako to a doctor of her choice.

Inasmuch as the new relationship was between father and son and would not involve the question of a stepmother, there would be no serious problems where Noboru was concerned. And since the boy worshipped Ryuji as a hero (and since he seemed to be basically a gentle man), they were certain to get along.

It would be a bad mistake to allow Ryuji to remain idle any longer. If Fusako intended to train Ryuji to take over Rex someday, she would be wise to start him learning the business and helping around the shop at once, particularly since Shibuya the manager was beginning to show his age.

Finally, though his gesture with the bankbook had made clear that there was nothing mercenary about Ryuji, the fact remained that the shipping slump had brought maritime stocks crashing, and it was obvious besides that he had been looking for a way out of his career as a seaman: Fusako would have to be careful not to compromise herself just because she was a widow. It was up to her to insist on an equal relationship, to make certain she was not being used.

Yoriko pressed each point home firmly but with patience, as if she were trying to persuade a child, though in fact Fusako was the older. Fusako was amazed to hear a woman she had considered a fool make such good sense.

"I never realized you were so"—there was new respect in her voice—"so capable."

"It's easy once you find out what they're up to. A year or so ago there was a man I thought I wanted to marry. And I told one of our producers the whole story. Maybe you've heard of him. Tatsuo Muragoshi? He's one of the best in the business. Anyway, it was just like him not to mention my work or my rating or even my contract. He just smiled the warmest smile you've ever seen and congratulated me and then he advised me to do all the things I've just told you to do. It seemed like such a nuisance, I left everything up to him. Well, in one week I found out that a certain person was seeing three women and had already fathered two bastards, and that wasn't all: he was sick, if you know what I mean. He had never held a decent job for long, and it looked like he was planning to kick the rest of my fam-

ily out as soon as we got married so he could sit around
swilling beer while I supported us. What do you think
about that? That's men for you. Not that there aren't
exceptions. . . ."

From that moment Fusako loathed the actress, and
her hatred was charged with the indignation of an honest, respectable bourgeois. She took Yoriko's unwitting
innuendo not only as an attack on Ryuji but also as an
insult to her own family and upbringing, and an affront
to the refined traditions of the Kuroda house which
amounted to a slur on her dead husband's honor.

In the first place, their backgrounds were entirely
different and there was no reason why her love affair
should develop in a pattern familiar to Yoriko. *Sooner
or later I'm going to have to make her understand.
There's nothing I can do now, though, because she's
just a customer, not a friend.*

Fusako didn't notice that the position she was taking in her rage was a contradiction of that violent
summer passion. Deep inside, she was angry not so
much for her dead husband as for the wholesome
household she had kept for herself and her son since his
death. And Yoriko's insinuation had sounded like the
thing she dreaded most, society's first thrust of reproach at her "indiscretion." Now, just as an appropriate "happy ending" was about to atone for that indiscretion, Yoriko had cast a pall over it. Purposely! Angry
for her dead husband, angry for the Kuroda house,

angry for Noboru—roiled by every anger that apprehension can breed, Fusako paled.

*If Ryuji were really an opportunist with all kinds of
dreadful secrets, I would never have fallen in love with
him. Yoriko may be a gullible fool, but I happen to
have a sound sense of what's good and what's bad.* The
thought was equivalent to a denial of that unaccount-
able summer passion, yet the whispering inside her
began suddenly to seethe, to swell until it threatened to
burst out.

Unaware of her friend's agitation, Yoriko sipped her
demitasse contentedly. Abruptly, as though she had remembered something, she set the cup in its saucer and,
turning back the cuff of her left sleeve, pointed to the
white inner side of her wrist.

"You must promise to keep this a secret. I wouldn't
tell anyone but you, Mama. It's the scar from that time
I was supposed to get married—I tried to kill myself
with a razor blade."

"That's strange—I don't remember seeing anything
about it in the papers," Fusako taunted, herself again.

"No, because Mr. Muragoshi ran all over the city
and managed to keep the news hushed up. But it bled
and bled."

Yoriko held her arm up in front of her and touched
her lips pityingly to the wrist before entrusting it to
Fusako for inspection. You had to look closely to see
them at all, a few irregular whitish scars that must

have been shallow, tentative cuts. Fusako felt only contempt. And she made a point of searching Yoriko's wrist
as though unable to locate the scars at all. Then she
knit sympathetic brows and said, becoming the proprietress of Rex again: "What a dreadful thing! Can
you imagine how many people all over Japan would
have wept if you'd succeeded. A lovely girl like you—
such a waste. Promise me you'll never do anything like
that again."

"Of course I won't, Mama, a stupid thing like that.
Those people you said would cry for me are all I have
to live for. Would you cry for me, Mama?"

"Crying wouldn't begin to be enough," Fusako
crooned, "but let's talk about something more pleasant."

Ordinarily, Fusako would have considered going to
a private detective agency an inauspicious beginning,
but now she was determined out of spite to receive a
favorable report from the same people who had
damned Yoriko's prospective husband.

"You know what?" she began. "I have to go up to
Tokyo with Mr. Shibuya tomorrow anyway, and when
we've finished what we have to do I think I'll get rid of
him and drop in at that investigation service you mentioned. If you could just write me a note of introduction?"

"Delighted." Yoriko took out the fountain pen she
had just bought and, fumbling through the contents of

her alligator pocketbook, came up with a small white
card.

A week and a day later Fusako had a long telephone
conversation with Yoriko. She sounded proud: "I just
wanted to call and thank you, I'm so grateful. I did just
as you suggested . . . yes, a great success. The report is
really very interesting. Thirty thousand yen is cheap
when you consider all the trouble they must have taken.
Would you like to hear it? I mean, do you have a minute? Do me a favor then and let me read it to you:

"'Special Investigation—Confidential Report. The
following are the findings of an investigation into the
affairs of Ryuji Tsukazaki as stipulated by the client.

"'One: particulars as indicated—subject's criminal
record, relations with women, etc. Particulars of the
subject's personal history coincide precisely with in-
formation in the client's possession. The mother, Ma-
sako, died when the subject was ten years of age. The
father, Hajime, was employed as a clerk in the Ka-
tsushita Ward Office in Tokyo. He did not remarry after
his wife's death, devoting himself to raising and educat-
ing his only son. The family home was destroyed in an
air raid in March of 1945. The subject's sister, Yoshiko,
died of typhus in May of the same year. The subject
graduated from the merchant-marine academy. . . .'

"It goes on and on that way. Isn't the writing terrible? Let me skip ahead: '. . . as for the subject's rela-

tions with women, he is not at present involved with a
woman nor is there any indication that he has ever
cohabited with a woman or even engaged in a pro-
longed or significant affair. . . .'

"That's really summing it up, wouldn't you say!

"'. . . though the subject displays slightly eccentric
tendencies, he is conscientious about his work, highly
responsible, and extremely healthy: he has never had a
serious illness. Results of the investigation to date show
no history of mental illness or other hereditary disease
in the immediate family. . . .'

"There was one more thing—yes, here it is: 'The
subject has no debts; he has never borrowed in advance
of his salary nor has he ever owed money to his employer. All indications point to a spotless financial
record. The subject is known to prefer solitude to company and has never been at ease socially; accordingly,
he does not always get along well with his col-
leagues. . . .'

"As long as we get along well that's all that matters.
Oh? Someone at the door? I'll let you go then. I just
wanted to thank you for being so very kind, I'm truly
grateful. I hope we'll be seeing you at the shop again
soon. . . . Ryuji? Yes, he's been coming in every day
since last week, just as you suggested. You know, getting to know his way around. You'll meet him next time
you come down . . . yes . . . yes, I will. And thanks
again. Goodbye."

CHAPTER FOUR

S CHOOL began on the eleventh but classes were over at noon. The gang hadn't met at all during the vacation. The chief hadn't even been in town: his parents had dragged him off on a sightseeing trip to Kyoto and Nara. Together again at last, they decided after eating lunch at school that the tip of Yamashita Pier, which was always deserted, would be a good place for a meeting.

"You guys probably think it's freezing out there. Everybody does, but they're all wrong," the chief announced. "There happens to be a very good windbreak. You'll see when we get there."

Since noon the sky had been cloudy and it was getting colder. The north wind, blowing down on them as they walked out along the pier, burned like icy fire.

Reclamation of the foreshore had been completed but one of the new docks was still under construction.

The sea was undulating grayly; three buoys, washed by endless waves, were bobbing up and down. The only distinct objects in the murky factory jungle across the harbor were the five smokestacks of an electric power plant; brackish yellow smoke struggled above the blurred line of factory rooftops. Beyond and far to the left of the dock, the pair of squat red-and-white lighthouses which formed the gateway to the harbor looked from here like a single column.

Moored at the dock in front of the shed to the right of them was a five- or six-ton freighter in terrible disrepair, a gray banner drooping from the stern. On the far side of the shed, in a berth they couldn't see, a foreign ship was apparently at anchor. Her beautiful white spars, which spired above the shed, were swaying, the only bright motion in the gloomy scene.

They saw immediately what the chief's windbreak was. Piled from the warehouse to the edge of the sea wall was a jumbled village of green-and-silver packing crates, each large enough to accommodate a small cow. Large plywood boxes begirt with tough steel bands and stamped with the names of foreign exporters, they had been left on the pier to rot.

The boys whooped down on the village and began a wild free-for-all, lurking between crates and leaping out in flying tackles or chasing each other in and out among the disordered rows. They were all in a sweat by the time the chief discovered at the very center of the village a large crate that was to his liking: two of the sides had fallen away but the steel band was still intact and the contents had been removed down to the last wisp of excelsior.

Shouting in a shrike's voice, the chief assembled the scattered band inside the crate. Three sat on the floor, three stood in the corners, arms resting on the steel band. They felt as if their outlandish vehicle was about to ascend on the arm of a crane into the cloudy winter sky.

Scribblings covered the plywood walls; they read each of them aloud: LET'S MEET IN YAMASHITA PARK— FORGET IT ALL AND TRY HAVING SOME FUN . . . like linked verses in a classical poem, each line was a clever distortion of the hopes and dreams in the preceding line: WE NEED TO FALL IN LOVE, PAL—FORGET WOMEN. WHO NEEDS THEM?—DON'T NEVER FORGET YOUR DREAM—GOT A BLACK SCAR ON MY BLUE BLUE HEART . . . peeking out of a corner was a young sailor's trembling soul: I HAVE CHANGED. I'M A NEW MAN. A freighter sketched in black let fly four arrow markers: the arrow at the left indicated YOKOHAMA, the arrow at the right, NEW YORK; the third arrow aspired to HEAVEN and the last plummeted toward HELL. Scrawled in English capitals and emphatically circled were the words ALL FORGET, and there was a self-portrait, a sailor with mournful eyes wearing a pea coat with upturned collar and smoking a seaman's pipe. The story was of the sailor's loneliness

and his longings, and it was told with self-importance
and overwhelming melancholy. Too typical to be true.
A sadly determined exaggeration of his qualifications
for dreaming about himself.

"This crap's all lies," the chief said angrily. Dou-
bling his powerless white hand into a fist he pummeled
the plywood wall. His small hand was for all of the
boys a symbol of despair. Now they were rejected even
by lies. But hadn't the chief said once that there was a
label called "impossibility" pasted all over the world,
that they were the only ones who could tear it off once
and for all?

"What's your hero been up to since last time? Well,
number three? There's a rumor going around that he's
come back. . . ." The chief felt every eye on him and his
voice was cold, venomous. As he spoke, he pulled out of
the pockets of his overcoat a pair of leather gloves and,
smoothing them over his fingers, turned back the cuffs
just enough so that the fluffy bright-red lining showed.

"He's back," Noboru admitted, wishing the subject
hadn't come up.

"And? Did he do anything *terrific* during this last
trip?"

"Well . . . yes! He ran into a hurricane in the Caribbean."

"Is that right! I suppose he got soaked like a
drowned rat? Like that time he took a shower in the
drinking fountain at the park?"

With that everyone laughed and kept laughing. Noboru knew he was being ridiculed, but he quickly regained his pride and was able to report on Ryuji's activities as though he were describing the habits of an insect.

The sailor had lolled around the house until the seventh. When Noboru learned that the *Rakuyo* had sailed on the fifth, he was stunned. This man so at one with the *Rakuyo*'s existence, so inseparably a part of the receding luster of a ship, had sundered himself from that beautiful whole, willfully banished from his dream the phantoms of ships and the sea!

Naturally Noboru stuck close to Ryuji during the vacation and listened to sea stories by the hour, gaining a knowledge of sailing none of the others could match. What he wanted, though, was not that knowledge but the green drop the sailor would leave behind when someday, in the very middle of a story, he started up in agitation and soared out to sea again.

The phantoms of the sea and ships and ocean voyages existed only in that glistening green drop. But with each new day, another of the fulsome odors of shore routine adhered to the sailor: the odor of home, the odor of neighbors, the odor of peace, odors of fish frying and pleasantries and furniture that never budged, the odor of household budget books and week-end excursions . . . all the putrid odors landsmen reek of, the stench of death.

Then began the laborious projects: Ryuji read the silly novels and art books Fusako recommended and he studied English conversation, a class each night on television and a text empty of nautical terms; he listened to Fusako lecture on problems of store management; he learned to wear the "smart" English clothes she lavished on him; he had suits tailored, and vests, and overcoats; and then, from the eighth of January, he began going in to the shop every day. That first morning, natty in a new suit of English tweed they had rushed to have ready in time, cheerful, expectant, eager. . . .

"Eager." Noboru spoke the word as though he had ice on the tip of his tongue.

"Eager," mimicked number two.

The boys stopped laughing as they listened. Gradually they realized how grave the situation was. It seemed to indicate the end of a dream they shared, a bleak, dreary future. And maybe they had been wrong: maybe there was no such thing as the ultimate after all.

Through a narrow gap between two crates, they glimpsed a motor launch knifing whitecaps as it angled across the harbor. The whine of the engine hovered over the water long after the boat was out of sight.

"Number three," the chief began, leaning languidly against the plywood wall, "would you like to make that sailor a hero again?"

Suddenly Noboru felt cold; he crouched and began

to toy with the pointed tips of his shoes. The answer when it finally came was an evasion: "But you know, he still keeps his sailor cap and his pea coat and even his dirty old turtleneck sweater folded away in his closet. You can tell he doesn't want to throw them away."

"There's just one way to make him a hero again," the chief continued, giving no indication that he had heard Noboru, "but I can't tell you what it is yet. The time will come, though, and soon."

The others were forbidden to probe for the answer when the chief chose to speak in riddles. Effortlessly changing the subject, he focused the conversation on himself.

"Let me tell you about my vacation. On this trip we took, I was rubbing noses with my folks every day from morning to night for the first time in quite a while. Fathers! Just think about it for a minute—they're enough to make you puke. Fathers are evil itself, laden with everything ugly in Man.

"There is no such thing as a good father because the role itself is bad. Strict fathers, soft fathers, nice moderate fathers—one's as bad as another. They stand in the way of our progress while they try to burden us with their inferiority complexes, and their unrealized aspirations, and their resentments, and their ideals, and the weaknesses they've never told anyone about, and their sins, and their sweeter-than-honey dreams, and the maxims they've never had the courage to live by—

they'd like to unload all that silly crap on us, all of it!
Even the most neglectful fathers, like mine, are no
different. Their consciences hurt them because they've
never paid any attention to their children and they
want the kids to understand just how bad the pain is—
to sympathize!

"On New Year's Day we went to Arashi Yama in
Kyoto and as we were crossing the Bridge of Moons I
asked my old man a question: 'Dad, is there any purpose in life?' You see what I was getting at, don't you,
what I really meant? *Father, can you give me one single reason why you go on living? Wouldn't it be better
just to fade away as quickly as possible?* But a first-
class insinuation never reaches a man like that. He just
looked surprised and his eyes bugged and he stared at
me. I hate that kind of ridiculous adult surprise. And
when he finally answered, what do you think he said?
'Son, nobody is going to provide you with a purpose in
life; you've got to make one for yourself.'

"How's that for a stupid, hackneyed moral! He just
pressed a button and out came one of the things fathers
are supposed to say. And did you ever look at a father's
eyes at a time like that? They're suspicious of anything
creative, anxious to whittle the world down into something puny they can handle. A father is a reality-
concealing machine, a machine for dishing up lies to
kids, and that isn't even the worst of it: secretly he
believes that he represents reality.

"Fathers are the flies of this world. They hover around our heads waiting for a chance, and when they see something rotten, they buzz in and root in it. Filthy, lecherous flies broadcasting to the whole world that they've screwed with our mothers. And there's nothing they won't do to contaminate our freedom and our ability. Nothing they won't do to protect the filthy cities they've built for themselves."

"My old man still won't buy me an air rifle," number two murmured, his arms around his knees.

"And he never will, either. But it's time you realized that a father who would buy you an air rifle is just as bad as one who won't."

"My father beat me again yesterday. That makes the third time since New Year's."

"Beat you?" Noboru repeated in horror.

"He slaps me across the face. Sometimes he even punches."

"Why don't you do something?"

"'Cause I'm not strong enough to take him."

"Then you should—why don't you"—Noboru's face was bright red and he was shouting—"butter his toast with potassium cyanide or something like that!"

"There are worse things than being beaten." The chief's thin red upper lip curled. "There are lots of things worse than that, only you don't know about them. You're one of the fortunate ones. When your father died your case became special. But you've got to know about the evil in the world too; otherwise you'll never have any real power."

"My old man is always coming home drunk and bullying my mother," number four said. "And when I stood up for her one time he got white as a sheet and grinned and said: 'Keep out of this. You want to take away your mother's pleasure?' But this time I've got something on him. He's got three mistresses."

"All my father ever does is pray to God," said number five.

Noboru asked what he prayed for.

"Well, the family's safety, peace on earth, prosperity—stuff like that. He thinks we're a model home or something. The bad part is he's even got my old lady thinking the same thing. The whole house is spic and span and everybody's supposed to be real honest and full of what he calls 'the good.' We even leave food out for the mice in the rafters so they won't have to sin by stealing. And you know what happens when dinner's over? Everybody hunches over and licks his plate clean so none of God's grace will be wasted."

"Does your old man make you do that too?"

"He never *makes* you do anything. He starts doing all this crappy stuff himself and everybody else is sort of in the habit of copying him. . . . You're really lucky, Noboru. You should be thankful."

Noboru was vexed at his immunity from the germs that infected the others, but at the same time he trem-

bled at the fragility of his chance good fortune. Some
providence he couldn't name had exempted him from
evil. His purity was as brittle as a new moon. His inno-
cence had sent an intricate net of feelers snaking toward the world, but when would they be snapped?
When would the world lose its vastness and lace him in
a strait jacket? That day, he knew, was not far away,
and even now he could feel a lunatic courage welling
within him. . . .

The chief had turned away so as not to see Noboru's
face. He was peering through a narrow gap in the
crates at the convolutions of the smoke and clouds
above the gray offing. He bit with small sharp shiny
teeth at the red lining of his leather gloves.

CHAPTER FIVE

H_{IS} mother's attitude changed. She became more affectionate, devoted more time to looking after his needs. Obviously this was the prelude to something he was going to find difficult to accept.

One evening Noboru had said good night and was on his way up to bed when Fusako climbed the stairs behind him, calling, with a key ring in her hand: "The key—I almost forgot the key!" In this he sensed something unnatural. She always came upstairs with him to lock his bedroom door and some nights she was gay and some nights sullen, but this was the first time she had ever made a speech about the key.

And then Ryuji, who was sitting in the living room in a maroon checked bathrobe reading a book called *The Reality of Merchandising*, looked up as though he had just happened to overhear, and called his mother's name.

"Yes, Ryuji?" she said, turning on the stairs. Noboru shuddered at the fawning sweetness in her voice.

"Don't you think it's time you stopped locking the boy's door? After all, Noboru's not a child any more and he knows what he should do and what he shouldn't. Isn't that right, Noboru?"

The large voice from the living room lumbered up the stairs. In the darkness at the top, Noboru froze like a small animal at bay, silent, his eyes gleaming. Fusako, who was maintaining a gentleness as smooth as oil, didn't even scold him for not answering.

"Well, I bet I know one happy young man around here," she said as she led him into his room. She checked the textbooks on his desk against a schedule of classes for the next day and examined the points on his pencils. Ryuji had been helping him with math every night and his grades had improved. Fusako's body, as she wandered around the room putting things in order, seemed so inordinately light and her movements so smooth that it was like watching an underwater dance. Finally she said good night and left. The long-familiar click of the lock never came.

As soon as he found himself alone, Noboru was uneasy. He had seen through the deceit. But there was no comfort in that at all.

It was a trap—a rabbit trap. The grownups expected the captive animal's rage and the familiar odors of his lair to transform themselves into the resignation and tolerance of a creature who has confined himself. A hideously subtle trap: the rabbit, ensnared, was no longer a rabbit.

His uneasiness at being in the unlocked room made him shiver even after he had buttoned his pajamas to the neck. They were beginning his education, a terrific, destructive education. Trying to force *maturity* on a thirteen-year-old boy. *Maturity* or, as the chief would call it, *perversion.* Noboru's feverish brain was pursuing an impossibility: *Is there no way that I can remain in the room and at the same time be out in the hall locking the door?*

A few days later he came home from school to find Ryuji and Fusako dressed for the evening and was told that they were all going out to see a movie. It was a seventy-millimeter spectacular Noboru had been wanting to see and he was very pleased.

After the movie they went to a restaurant in Chinatown and had dinner in a small private room upstairs. Noboru loved Chinese food; and he liked the dish-laden wooden tray which spun around and around in the center of the table.

When all the food had been brought to the table, Ryuji signaled Fusako with his eyes. Apparently she was not prepared to face the moment sober: she had been sipping Chinese Lao-chu wine and already her eyes were a little red.

Noboru had never received such cordial treatment from the adults, nor had he ever seen them so ridiculously hesitant in his presence. It seemed to be some special adult ritual. He knew what they were going to say and it interested him very little. But he did enjoy watching them handle him from across the table as though he were a vulnerable, easily frightened, and all-unknowing little bird—that was a real spectacle. They had laid the tender, down-ruffled little bird on a platter and appeared now to be pondering a way to eat out its heart without causing it distress.

Noboru didn't really object to the darling image of himself he knew Ryuji and his mother entertained in their imaginations. He would just have to be careful to look victimized.

"Noboru dear, I want you to listen carefully to what Mother is going to say because it's something very important," Fusako began finally. "You're going to have a papa again. Mr. Tsukazaki is going to be your new father."

As he listened Noboru succeeded in keeping his face a blank, and he was confident that he looked utterly bewildered. So far, so good. But he hadn't counted on the incredible nonsense that followed:

"Your real papa was a wonderful man. You were eight years old when he passed away, so you must remember him and miss him very much. But I can't tell you how lonely Mother has been these past five years, and I know you've been lonely too. And you must have thought lots of times that both of us needed a new papa. I want you to understand, dear, how much I've wanted a strong, gentle, wonderful papa for both our sakes. And it's been all the harder because your father was such a fine, honest man. But you're a grownup now, so I know you'll understand: how hard these five years have been, and how lonely, with just the two of us. . . ." She fumbled an imported handkerchief out of her purse and began to cry: it was really very silly.

"Everything I've done has been for you, dear— everything. There isn't another man in this world as strong and as gentle and as wonderful in every way as Mr. Tsukazaki. Noboru, I want you to call Mr. Tsuka-zaki Papa now; we're going to be married early next month and we'll invite lots of friends and have a lovely party."

Ryuji had averted his eyes from Noboru's impassive face and was engrossed in drinking, adding crystal sugar to the Lao-chu wine, stirring, tossing off the cup, and pouring himself another. He was afraid of seeming brazen to the boy.

Noboru knew that he was being feared as well as pitied, and the gentle threat had made him drunk: when he leveled the full iciness of his heart at the adults, a smile was playing at the corners of his mouth. It was hardly more than a wisp of a smile, the kind you see on the face of a schoolboy who has come to class unprepared but cocksure as a man leaping off a cliff; and yet, on the other side of the red formica table, Ryuji saw it out of the corner of his eye and snatched it up. Again, a misunderstanding. The grin he flashed back was the same brand of exaggerated glee as his smile that day near the park when, to Noboru's intense disappointment and humiliation, he had appeared in a dripping-wet shirt.

"Fair enough. Then I won't call you Noboru any more. From now on, it's Son. What do you say, Son. Shake hands with Dad." Ryuji placed one hard open hand on the table; Noboru struggled toward it as though he were paddling under water. No matter how he stretched, Ryuji's fingers seemed just beyond reach. At last their hands met, thick fingers grappled his own, and the hot, calloused handshake began. Noboru felt a whirlwind catch him up and spin him away toward the tepid, formless world he dreaded most. . . .

That night, as soon as Fusako had left his room and closed the door without locking it, Noboru's head began to swim. Hard heart . . . hard heart: he tried repeating the words to himself, but that only made him want to hold the genuine article in his hand. Hard as an iron anchor. . . .

Before leaving the room, his mother had turned off the gas heater. Now heat and cold were mingled in a fold of tepid air. If he could just brush his teeth, put on his pajamas in a hurry, and bundle into bed, he would be all right.

But an evasive languor made even removing his turtleneck sweater seem a wearisome task. Never had he waited so anxiously for his mother to reappear, to come back to his room, for example, to mention something she had forgotten to say. Nor had he ever felt such contempt for her.

He waited in the gradually mounting cold. And, weary of waiting, he abandoned himself to an absurd fantasy. His mother had come back and she was shouting: *It was all a lie. I'm so sorry to have made a game out of fooling you. Will you forgive me? We are most certainly not going to get married. If we did a thing like that the world would turn to chaos: ten tankers would sink in the harbor, and a thousand trains would be derailed; the glass in the windows all over the city would shatter, and every lovely rose would turn black as coal.*

But she did not come back and finally Noboru contrived a situation in which her return would mean real trouble. He could no longer distinguish cause from effect: possibly this unreasonable yearning for his mother was due to a desire to wound her even if he had to share the pain.

The courage propelling him now was frightening: his hands began to temble. He hadn't touched the dresser since the night Fusako had stopped locking his door. There was a reason: shortly after Ryuji's return on the morning of December 30, he had observed them through the peephole and managed to watch the progression of merging shapes to its dazzling climax; but the danger in sneaking into the wall in broad daylight, with the door not even locked, had discouraged him from risking the adventure again.

But now he felt like invoking curses, and longed for a small revolution. If he were really a genius and the world mere emptiness, then why shouldn't he have the ability to prove it? He would have only to open a tiny crack in the glossy teacup of a world the adults believed in.

Noboru bolted to the dresser and seized the handle. Ordinarily he removed the drawer as quietly as possible but this time he wrenched it loose and dropped it to the floor. Then he stood and listened. Not a sound in response from anywhere in the house, no footsteps thudding up the stairs, nothing. The stillness drowned out everything but the pounding in his chest.

Noboru looked at his watch. It was only ten o'clock. Then a strange plot took shape in his mind: he would do his homework inside the dresser. The irony was beautiful, and what better way to mock the meanness of their suspicions?

Taking a flashlight and some English word cards, he

wriggled into the chest. A mysterious force would draw his mother to the room. She would find him in the chest and guess his purpose. Shame and rage would inflame her. She would haul him out of the dresser and slap his face; then he would show her the word cards and protest, with eyes as innocent as a lamb's: "But what did I do wrong? I was only studying. It's easier to concentrate in a small space. . . ." He stopped imagining the episode and laughed out loud, gasping in the dusty air.

The moment he huddled inside the chest he was calm again. The trembling and the trepidation seemed almost funny now; he even had a feeling he would be able to study well. Not that it really mattered: this was the world's outer edge. So long as he was here, Noboru was in contact with the naked universe. No matter how far you ran, escape beyond this point was impossible.

Bending his arms in the cramped space, he began to read the cards in the light of the flashlight.

abandon

> By now this word was an old acquaintance: he knew it well.

ability

> Was that any different from *genius?*

aboard

> A ship again; he recalled the loudspeaker ringing across the deck that day when

Ryuji sailed. And then the colossal, golden horn, like a proclamation of despair.

absence
absolute

He didn't even turn off the flashlight, sinking, before he knew it, into sleep.

It was close to midnight when Ryuji and Fusako went up to the bedroom. The announcement at dinner had relieved them of a great weight and they felt that a new phase was beginning.

But when it was time to go to bed, a strange shame stirred in Fusako. All evening she had discussed matters of importance, touched too lingeringly on the emotions of kinship, and now, in addition to a deep sense of quiet and relief, she felt embarrassed in the presence of something she couldn't name, something unaccountably sacred.

Choosing a black negligee she knew Ryuji liked, Fusako got into bed and, disregarding for the first time Ryuji's preference for a brightly lighted room, asked him to turn out all the lights. He embraced her in the dark.

When it was done Fusako said: "I thought I wouldn't feel embarrassed if all the lights were out, but it was just the opposite. The darkness becomes a huge eye and you feel as if you're being watched the whole time."

Ryuji laughed at her nervousness and glanced around the room. The curtains on the windows shut out all the light from the street. The gas heater burning in one corner gave off a pale reflection of bluish light. It was just like the night sky above a small distant city. The frail luster of the brass bedposts trembled in the darkness.

Then Ryuji's eye fell on the wainscot along the wall adjoining the next room. From one spot on the ornately carved wooden border, light was trickling into the room.

"I wonder what that is," he mused aloud. "Do you think Noboru's still up? You know, this place is getting pretty run-down. I'd better seal that up in the morning."

Like a serpent coiling for a strike, Fusako lifted her bare white neck from the bed and peered through the darkness at the point of light. She comprehended with terrific speed. One motion carried her out of bed and into a dressing gown; then she bolted from the room without a word. Ryuji called after her but there was no answer.

He heard Noboru's door open. Silence. A muffled sound that might have been Fusako crying: Ryuji slid out of bed. He paced the floor in the darkness trying to decide whether he should go straight in or wait and finally, sitting down on the couch near the window, lit a cigarette.

Noboru started awake as something ferociously strong hauled him out of the dresser by the seat of his pants. For a minute, he didn't realize what had happened. His mother's slender, supple hands were falling on his nose and lips and mouth and he couldn't hold his eyes open. It was the first time she had ever laid a hand on him.

He lay almost prostrate on the floor, one of his legs thrust into a tangle of shirts and underwear scattered when they had stumbled over the drawer. He hadn't imagined his mother could muster such terrific strength.

Finally he managed to look up at the panting figure glaring down at him.

The skirts of her dark-blue robe were wide open, the fleshy swells of her lower body looked grotesquely massive and threatening. Soaring high above the gradually tapering trunk was her face, gasping, grieved, turned horribly old in an instant and drenched in tears. The bulb on the distant ceiling wreathed her bedraggled hair with a lunatic halo.

All this Noboru took in at a glance and at the back of his icy brain a memory stirred: it was as if he had participated in this same moment a long time ago. This, beyond a doubt, was the punishment scene he had watched so often in his dreams.

His mother began to sob and, still glaring down at him through her tears, screamed in tones he could scarcely understand: "It's humiliating—it's just so humiliating! My own son, a filthy, disgusting thing like that—I could die this very minute! Oh, Noboru, how could you have done this to me!"

To his surprise, Noboru discovered that he had lost all desire to protest that he had been studying English. But that didn't make any difference now. Obviously, his mother was not mistaken; and she had brushed against "reality," a thing she dreaded worse than leeches. In one sense, that made them more nearly equal now than they had ever been: it was almost empathy. Pressing his palms to his reddened, burning cheeks, Noboru resolved to watch carefully how a person drawn so near could retreat in one fleeting instant to an unattainable distance. Clearly it was not the discovery of reality itself that had spawned her indignation and her grief: Noboru knew that his mother's shame and her despair derived from a kind of prejudice. She had been quick to interpret the reality, and inasmuch as her banal interpretation was the cause of all her agitation, no clever excuse from him would be to any purpose.

"I'm afraid this is more than I can handle," Fusako said finally, her voice ominously quiet. "A frightening child like this is too much for me. . . . You just wait a minute! I'm going to see that Father punishes you so that you won't dare think of this kind of thing again." It was clear that Fusako expected her threat to make Noboru cry and apologize.

But then her resolution faltered; for the first time,

she considered dealing with the problem later. If she could get Noboru to apologize before Ryuji came into the room, she would be able to hide the details from him and save her pride as a mother. Then the tears and the apology would have to come quickly; but she couldn't suggest that mother and son conspire to resolve the problem, for she had threatened that the father would punish him. She could only wait in silence.

But Noboru didn't say a word. He was interested only in the ultimate destination of the great engine now in motion. In that dark hole inside the chest he had stood at the outermost limit of his world, at the edge of the seas and the deserts. And because all things took life there, because he was to be punished for having been there, he could not return to the tepid towns of men, nor lower his face to their tear-moistened lawns. On the oath he had sworn to that beautiful pinnacle of humanity swathed in the roar of that horn, sworn to the gleaming representatives of order he had seen through the peephole that summer night, he could never turn back again.

The door opened tentatively and Ryuji peeked into the room.

Fusako saw that she and her son had lost an opportunity, and she grew angry again. Either Ryuji should have stayed away altogether or he should have come in with her at the beginning.

Irritated by Ryuji's clumsy entrance and struggling

to align her feelings, Fusako became more furiously angry at Noboru than before.

"Would you mind telling me what's going on here?" Ryuji said as he came into the room.

"I want you to punish him, Father. If this child isn't beaten within an inch of his life the evil in him will keep getting worse. He was spying on us through a hole in the chest there."

"Is that right, Son?" There was no anger in Ryuji's voice.

Still sprawled on the floor, his legs flung out in front of him, Noboru nodded.

"I see. . . . Well, I suppose the idea just sort of hit you all of a sudden and you tried it tonight?"

Noboru shook his head emphatically.

"Oh? Then you've done the same thing maybe once or twice before?"

Again Noboru shook his head.

"Then this has been going on from the very beginning?"

Seeing the boy nod, Fusako and Ryuji exchanged involuntary glances. Noboru had a pleasant vision of the lightning in the adults' gaze illuminating the life on shore that Ryuji dreamed about and Fusako's wholesome household as they crashed noisily into rubble—but his excitement had led him to overestimate the power of his imagination. He had been expecting an impassioned reaction.

"I see" was all Ryuji said. His hands were stuffed into the pockets of his bathrobe. The hairy legs protruding below the robe were directly in front of Noboru's face.

Now Ryuji was obliged to reach a father's decision, the first decision about shore life he had ever been forced to make. But his memory of the sea's fury was tempering his critical notons of land and the landsman with inordinate mildness, and his instinctive approach to problems was therefore thwarted. To beat the boy would be easy enough, but a difficult future awaited him. He would have to receive their love with dignity, to deliver them from daily dilemmas, to balance daily accounts; he was expected in some vague, general way to comprehend the incomprehensible feelings of the mother and the child and to become an infallible teacher, perceiving the causes of a situation even as unconscionable as this one: he was dealing here with no ocean squall but the gentle breeze that blows ceaselessly over the land.

Though Ryuji didn't realize it, the distant influence of the sea was at work on him again: he was unable to distinguish the most exhaulted feelings from the meanest, and suspected that essentially important things did not occur on land. No matter how hard he tried to reach a realistic decision, shore matters remained suffused with the hues of fantasy.

In the first place, it would be a mistake to interpret

literally Fusako's plea that he beat Noboru. Sooner or later, he knew, she would come to feel grateful for his leniency. Besides, he found himself believing in the paternal instinct. As he hurried to banish from his mind merely dutiful concern for this reticent, precocious, bothersome child, this boy whom he didn't really love, Ryuji managed to convince himself that he was brimming with genuine fatherly affection. It seemed to him besides that he was discovering the emotion for the first time, and he was surprised at the unpredictability of his affections.

"I see," he said again, lowering himself slowly to the floor and crossing his legs.

"You sit down too, Mother. I've been thinking, and it seems to me that Noboru isn't the only one to blame for what's happened. When I came into this house, Son, your life changed too. Not that it was wrong for me to come, but your life *did* change, and it's natural for a boy in junior high school to feel curious about changes in his life. What you did was wrong, there's no question about that, but from now on I want you to direct that curiosity toward your school work, do you understand?

"You have nothing to say about what you saw. And nothing to ask. You're not a child any more and someday we'll be able to laugh together and talk about what's happened here as three adults. Mother, I want you to calm down too. We're going to forget about the past and face the future happily, hand in hand. I'll seal that hole up in the morning and then we can all forget this whole unpleasant evening. Right? What do you say, Noboru?"

Noboru listened feeling as though he were about to suffocate. *Can this man be saying things like that? This splendid hero who once shone so brightly?*

Every word burned like fire. He wanted to scream, as his mother had screamed: *How can you do this to me?* The sailor was saying things he was never meant to say. Ignoble things in wheedling, honeyed tones, fouled words not meant to issue from his lips until Doomsday, words such as men mutter in stinking lairs. And he was speaking proudly, for he believed in himself, was satisfied with the role of father he had stepped forward to accept.

He is satisfied. Noboru felt nauseous. Tomorrow Ryuji's slavish hands, the hands of a father puttering over carpentry of a Sunday afternoon, would close forever the narrow access to that unearthly brilliance which he himself had once revealed.

"Right? What do you say, Son?" Ryuji concluded, clapping a hand on Noboru's shoulder. He tried to shake free and couldn't. He was thinking that the chief had been right: there were worse things than being beaten.

CHAPTER SIX

Noboru asked the chief
to call an emergency meeting: on their way home from
school, the boys convened at the swimming pool next to
the foreign cemetery.

Climbing down a horse's back of a hill thick with
giant oaks was one way to reach the pool. At midslope
they stopped and gazed through the evergreen trees at
the cemetery below: quartz sparkled in the winter
light.

From this point on the hill, the tombstones and
stone crosses ranged in long terraced rows were all facing away from them. The inky green of sago palm
bloomed among the graves; greenhouse flower cuttings
laid in the shadows of stone crosses brightened the
lawn with unseasonable reds and greens.

Above the rooftops in the valley loomed the Marine
Tower, the foreigners' graves lay to the right, and in a

smaller valley to the left, the pool waited. In the off season, the bleachers there made an excellent meeting place.

Tripping over bared tree roots which swelled like tumid black blood vessels across the face of the slope, the boys scrambled down the hill and broke onto the withered grass path that led into the evergreens surrounding the pool. The pool was drained, and very quiet. The blue paint on the bottom was chipping; dry leaves had piled up in the corners. The blue steel ladder stopped far short of the bottom. Banking into the west now, the sun was hidden behind the cliffs which enclosed the valley like folding screens: dusk had come already to the bottom of the pool.

Noboru trailed along behind the others: he could still see in his mind the backs of all those endless foreign graves—graves and crosses all turned away from him. Then what would this place in back be called, this place where they were?

They sat in a diamond on the blackened concrete bleachers. Noboru took out of his briefcase a slim notebook and handed it to the chief without a word. Inked on the cover in venomous red was: "Charges against Ryuji Tsukazaki."

Craning their necks to see, the boys read the text together. It was an excerpt from Noboru's diary; the dresser-drawer incident of the night before brought to eighteen the number of entries.

"This is awful," the chief mourned. "This last one alone is worth about thirty-five points. And the total—let's see—even if you go easy and call this first charge five points, they get worse the closer they get to the end: I'm afraid the total's way over a hundred and fifty. I didn't realize it was quite this bad. We're going to have to do something about this."

As he listened to the chief, Noboru began to tremble. Finally he asked: "Is there any chance of saving him?"

"None at all. It's too bad, though."

A long silence followed. This the chief interpreted as indicating a lack of courage and he began to speak again, twisting between his fingers the tough vein of a dried leaf he had pulverized: "All six of us are geniuses. And the world, as you know, is empty. I know I've said this before, but have you ever thought about it carefully? Because to assume for those reasons that we are permitted to do anything we want is sloppy thinking. As a matter of fact, we are the ones who do the permitting. Teachers, schools, fathers, society—we permit all those garbage heaps. And not because we're powerless either. Permitting is our special privilege and if we felt any pity at all we wouldn't be able to permit this ruthlessly. What it amounts to is that we are constantly permitting unpermissible things. There are only a very few really permissible things: like the sea, for example—"

"And ships," Noboru added.

"Right—anyway, very few. And if they conspire against us, it's just as if your own dog were to bite a hunk out of your hand. It's a direct insult to our special privilege."

"We've never done anything about it before," interrupted number one.

"That doesn't mean we're never going to," the chief answered adroitly, his voice benign. "But getting back to Ryuji Tsukazaki," he continued, "he's never meant much to the group as a whole, but for number three he was a person of considerable importance. At least he's credited with having shown number three some luminous evidence of the internal order of life I've mentioned so often. But then he betrayed number three. He became the worst thing on the face of this earth, a father. And something has to be done. It would have been much better if he'd just stayed the useless sailor he started out to be.

"As I've said before, life consists of simple symbols and decisions. Ryuji may not have have known it, but he was one of those symbols. At least, according to number three s testimony it *seems* that he was.

"I'm sure you all know where our duty lies. When a gear slips out of place it's our job to force it back into position. If we don't, order will turn to chaos. We all know that the world is empty and that the important thing, the only thing, is to try to maintain order in that emptiness. And so we are guards, and more than that because we also have executive power to insure that order is maintained."

The chief stated the conclusion simply: "We'll have to pass sentence. In the long run it's for his own good. Number three! Do you remember that day on the pier when I said there was only one way to make him a hero again, and that soon I'd be able to tell you what it was?"

"I remember," Noboru answered, trying to keep his legs from trembling.

"Well, the time has come."

The other boys sought each other's faces, then sat motionless and silent. They understood the grave importance of what the chief was about to say.

They gazed into the empty, dusk-shadowed pool. White lines were painted on the chipped blue bottom. The dry leaves in the corners had sifted in like dust.

At that moment, the pool was terrifically deep. Deeper and deeper as watery blue darkness seeped up from the bottom. The knowledge, so certain it was sensuous, that nothing was there to support the body if one plunged in generated around the empty pool an unremitting tension. Gone now was the soft summer water that received the swimmer's body and bore him lightly afloat, but the pool, like a monument to summer and to water, had endured, and it was dangerous, lethal.

The blue steel ladder crept over the edge and down into the pool and, still far from the bottom, stopped. Nothing there to support a body, nothing at all!

"Classes are over at two tomorrow; we can have him meet us here and then take him out to our dry dock at Sugita. Number three, it's up to you to lure him down here somehow.

"I'm going to give the rest of you instructions now. Please remember what you're supposed to bring. I'll take care of the sleeping pills and the scalpel myself. We won't be able to handle a powerful man like that unless we knock him out first. Adults are supposed to take one to three tablets of that German stuff we've got at home, so he should go out like a light if we give him about seven. I'll make powder out of the tablets so they'll dissolve quicker in tea.

"Number one, you're to bring some six-foot lengths of strong hemp rope; you'd better have—let's see—one, two, three, four—make it five lengths just to be sure. Number two, you prepare a thermos of hot tea and hide it in your briefcase. Since number three has the job of getting him down here, he doesn't have to bring anything. We'll need sugar and spoons, and paper cups for us and a dark-colored plastic cup for him—that'll be your job, number four. Number five, you get some cloth for a blindfold and a towel we can use for a gag.

"You can each bring any kind of cutting tool you like—knives, saws, whatever you prefer.

"We've already practiced the essentials on a cat and this'll be the same, so there's nothing to worry about. The job's a little bigger this time, that's all—and it may stink a little worse."

The boys sat dumb as stones and stared into the empty pool.

"Are you scared, number one?" Number one managed a slight shake of his head.

"How about you, number two?" As though suddenly cold, the boy stuffed his hands into his overcoat pockets.

"What's wrong, number three?" Noboru was gasping for breath, his mouth utterly dry as if stuffed with straw: he couldn't answer.

"That's what I was afraid of. You're all great talkers, but when the chips are down you haven't got one thimbleful of nerve. Well, maybe this will make you feel better; I brought it along just in case." The chief produced from his briefcase an ocher lawbook and deftly flipped it open to the page he wanted.

"I want all of you to listen carefully: 'Penal Code, Article Fourteen,'" he read. "'*Acts of juveniles less than fourteen years of age are not punishable by law.*' I'll read it again as loud as I can: '*Acts of juveniles less than fourteen years of age are not punishable by law.*'"

The chief had the others pass the book around while he continued: "You might say that our fathers and the fictitious society they believe in passed this law for our benefit. And I think we should be grateful to them. This law is the adults' way of expressing the high hopes they have for us. But it also represents all the dreams they've never been able to make come true. They've assumed just because they've roped themselves so tight they can't even budge that we must be helpless too; they've been careless enough to allow us here, and only here, a glimpse of blue sky and absolute freedom.

"This law they've written is a kind of nursery tale, a pretty deadly nursery tale, I'd say. And in a way it's understandable. After all, up to now we *have* been nursery kids, adorable, defenseless, innocent kids.

"But three of us here will be fourteen next month—myself, number one, and you, number three. And you other three will be fourteen in March. Just think about it a minute. This is our last chance!"

The chief scrutinized their faces and saw tension easing out of their cheeks, fear dwindling away. Awakening for the first time to society's sweet cordiality, the boys felt secure in the knowledge that their enemies were actually their protectors.

Noboru looked up at the sky. Afternoon blue was fading into the sifting grays of dusk. Suppose Ryuji tried at the height of his heroic death throes to look up at this hallowed sky? It seemed a shame to blindfold him.

"This is our last chance," the chief repeated. "If we

don't act now we will never again be able to obey freedom's supreme command, to perform the deed essential to filling the emptiness of the world, unless we are prepared to sacrifice our lives. And you can see that it's absurd for the executioners to risk their own lives. If we don't act now we'll never be able to steal again, or murder, or do any of the things that testify to man's freedom. We'll end up puking flattery and gossip, trembling our days away in submission and compromise and fear, worrying about what the neighbors are doing, living like squealing mice. And someday we'll get married, and have kids, and finally we'll become fathers, the vilest things on earth!

"We must have blood! Human blood! If we don't get it this empty world will go pale and shrivel up. We must drain that sailor's fresh lifeblood and transfuse it to the dying universe, the dying sky, the dying forests, and the drawn, dying land.

"Now! The time is now! In another month they'll have finished clearing the land around our dry dock and then the place will fill up with people. Besides, we're almost fourteen."

The chief glanced through a black frame of evergreen branches at the watery gray sky and observed: "Looks like tomorrow will be a nice day."

CHAPTER SEVEN

Oɴ the morning of the twenty-second, Fusako went with Ryuji to City Hall to ask the Mayor of Yokohama if he would be toastmaster at their wedding dinner. He said he would be honored. On the way back, they stopped at a department store and ordered engraved wedding announcements. Reservations for the reception had already been made at the New Grand Hotel. After an early lunch downtown, they returned to Rex.

Just after one, Ryuji left the shop to keep an appointment he had mentioned earlier in the day. A high-school classmate who was now a First Officer had docked that morning at Takashima Pier and was free to meet him only in the early afternoon. And Ryuji didn't want to appear in an expensive English suit. He didn't like the idea of flaunting his new circumstances in front of an old friend; at least not until after the wedding. He would stop at the house on his way to the dock and change into his old seaman's clothes.

"Are you sure I don't have to worry that you'll get on that ship and disappear?" Fusako teased as she accompanied him to the door.

Noboru, pretending to need help with homework, had summoned Ryuji conspiratorially to his room the night before and entrusted him with a mission which he was discharging faithfully:

"Dad, all the guys are looking forward to hearing some of your sea stories tomorrow afternoon. We're going to meet on that hill above the pool when school gets out at two. Everybody's been wanting to meet you and I promised you'd come. You will, won't you? And tell them some of your adventures? And would you wear your sailor clothes like you used to, and your sailor cap? Only it's got to be a secret from Mom. You could tell her you're going to meet an old friend or something and get off work early."

This was the first son-to-father favor Noboru had ever asked and Ryuji was determined not to betray the boy's trust. It was a father's duty. Even if the truth got out later it would only mean having a good laugh together, so he had fabricated a plausible story and left the shop early.

Ryuji was sitting on the roots of a giant oak near the top of the hill when the boys appeared just after two. One of them, a boy with crescent eyebrows and red lips who seemed particularly bright, thanked him politely for having come, and then suggested that a more suitable spot for his talk would be what he called their dry dock. Supposing they were headed somewhere near the harbor, Ryuji agreed to go.

It was a mild midwinter afternoon. The shade was chilly but in the sun, which reached them through a wispy layer of cloud, they didn't need their overcoats. Ryuji was wearing his gray turtleneck sweater and carried his pea coat over his arm; the six boys, each with a briefcase, anticked around him as he walked along, now surging ahead, now falling behind. For this generation, they were smallish boys: the scene reminded Ryuji of six tugboats laboring futilely to tow a freighter out to sea. He didn't notice that their frolicking had a kind of frenzied uneasiness.

The boy with the crescent eyebrows informed him they were going to take a streetcar. Ryuji was surprised, but he made no objection: he understood that the setting for a story was important to boys this age. No one made a move to get off until the last stop at Sugita, which was far south of the city.

"Say, where are you guys taking me?" he asked repeatedly, as though amused. He had determined to spend a day with the boys and it wouldn't do to appear annoyed, no matter what happened.

Though careful not to draw attention to the fact, he was observing Noboru constantly. As the boy mingled happily with his friends, Ryuji saw the piercing look of cross-examination go out of his eyes for the first time. It was like watching motes of dust dance into color in the winter light streaming through the streetcar window: borders betwen Noboru and the others became blurred, and he confused them. That had hardly seemed possible, not with a boy so different from everyone else, a lonely boy with a peculiar habit of eying adults furtively. And it proved that Ryuji had been right to take off half a day in order to amuse Noboru and his friends. Right, he knew, in terms of a father's moral obligation. Most books and magazines would agree. Noboru had approached voluntarily and offered in this excursion a providential opportunity to cement their relationship. It was a chance for a father and son originally strangers to forge a bond of deep and tender trust stronger than mere blood ties could ever be. And since Ryuji could very well have become a father when he was twenty, there was nothing out of the ordinary about Noboru's age.

As soon as they were off the streetcar, the boys began tugging Ryuji toward a road which wound into the hills. "Hey, wait a minute," he protested. "I never heard of a dry dock in the mountains!"

"No? But in Tokyo the subway runs up above your head!"

"I can see I'm no match for you guys." Ryuji winced, and the boys howled, thoroughly pleased with themselves.

The road skirted the ridge of Aoto Hill and entered

Kanazawa Ward. They passed an electric power plant with its webs of power lines and gnarled porcelain insulators thrown up against the winter sky, then entered Tomioka Tunnel. Emerging on the other side, they saw glinting along the ridge to the right the tracks of the Tokyo–Yokohama express; bright new housing lots covered the slope to the left.

"Almost there now. We go up between those lots. All this used to be an American Army installation." The boy who seemed to be their leader tossed the explanation over one shoulder and stepped ahead; his manner and language, in a matter of minutes, had become brusque.

Work on the lots had been completed; there were even stone boundary fences and the skeletons of more than a few houses. Surrounding Ryuji, the six boys marched straight up the road that ran between the lots. Near the top of the hill, the road abruptly disappeared and there began a terrace of uncultivated fields. It was like clever sleight of hand: a man standing at the bottom of the hill would never guess that the straight, well-graded road gave way at this point on the slope to a grassy wilderness.

There wasn't a person in sight. The heavy droning of bulldozers echoed from the other side of the hill. Sounds of automobile traffic ascended from the tunnel road far below. Except for the echoes of engine noise, the vast landscape was empty and the sounds themselves only heightened the bright desolation.

Here and there wooden stakes thrust up from the meadow: they were beginning to rot. A footpath buried under fallen leaves skirted the ridge of the hill. They crossed the withered field. Just off to the right, a rusted water tank surrounded by a tangle of barbed wire lay half buried in the ground: bolted lopsidedly to the tank was a sheet of rusting tin lettered in English. Ryuji stopped and read the notice:

U. S. Forces Installation
Unauthorized Entry Prohibited and Punishable
under Japanese Law

"What's 'punishable' mean?" the leader asked There was something about the boy Ryuji didn't like. The flicker of light in his eye when he asked the question suggested that he knew the answer perfectly well. Ryuji forced himself to explain politely.

"Oh—but this isn't army property any more, so I guess we can do whatever we want. Look!" Even as he spoke the boy appeared to have forgotten the subject, as though it were a balloon he had abandoned to the sky.

"Here's the top."

Ryuji stepped to the summit and gazed at the panorama stretching below. "You've got yourselves quite a place here."

The hill overlooked the northeastern sea. Away to the left, bulldozers were cutting a red-loam slope into the side of a cliff and dump trucks were hauling the earth away. Distance dwarfed the trucks but the roar of their engines battered endless waves into the choppy air. Further down in the valley were the gray roofs of an industrial laboratory and an airplane factory: in the concrete garden in front of the central offices, one small pine was bathed in sun.

Around the factory curled an isolated country village. The thin winter sunlight accented the highs and lows in the rows of rooftops and corrected the files of shadow cast by countless ridgepoles. The objects glinting like seashells through the thin smoke covering the valley were automobile windows.

As it neared the sea, the landscape appeared to fold in on itself and assumed a special quality of rust, and sadness, and clutter. Beyond a tangle of rusted machinery discarded on the beach, a vermilion crane swung in wobbly arcs, and beyond the crane, there was the sea, the piled white of stone breakwaters and, at the edge of the reclaimed foreshore, a green dredger smoking blackly.

The sea made Ryuji feel that he had been away from it a long, long time. Fusako's bedroom overlooked the harbor but he never went near the window any more. The water, with spring still far away, was Prussian blue except where the shadow of one pearly cloud

turned it pale, chilly white. The rest of the midafter-
noon sky was cloudless, a bleached, monotone blue fading where it neared the horizon.

The sea spread from the dirtied shore toward the
offing like a huge ocher net. There were no ships close
in to shore; several freighters were moving across the
offing, small vessels and obviously, even at this distance, antique.

"The ship I was on was no little tug like that."

"I'll say—the *Rakuyo* had a displacement of ten
thousand tons," Noboru affirmed. He had spoken hardly
a word all afternoon.

"C'mon, let's go," the leader urged, tugging at
Ryuji's sleeve. Descending the footpath a short distance, they came to a segment of land miraculously
untouched by the surrounding devastation, a vestige of
the mountaintop as it must once have been. The clearing, on one of a twisting series of slopes sheltered from
the east wind by a stand of oak and protected to the
west by the heavily wooded hilltop, merged into a neglected field of winter rye. Withered vines snaked
through the underbrush around the path; sitting at the
tip of one was a shriveled, blood-red gourd. Sunlight
out of the western sky was thwarted the moment it
descended here: a few pale beams flickered over the
tips of dead leaves.

Ryuji, though he remembered having done similar
things in his own youth, marveled at a young boy's

unique ability to discover this sort of hiding place and make it his own.

"Which one of you guys found this place?"

"I did. But I live right over in Sugita. I pass by here lots of times on the way to school. I found it and showed the other guys."

"And where's this dry dock of yours?"

"Over here." The leader was standing in front of a small cave shadowed by the hilltop, smiling as he pointed at the entrance.

To Ryuji the smile seemed as brittle as fine glass crystal and very dangerous. He couldn't say why he thought so. With the adroitness of a minnow slipping through a net, the boy shifted his gaze away from Ryuji's face and continued the explanation.

"This is our dry dock. A dry dock on top of a mountain. We repair run-down ships here, dismantle them first and then rebuild them from the ground up."

"Is that right? . . . Must be quite a job hauling a ship way up here."

"It's easy—nothing to it," the boy said, and the too pretty smile lit his face again.

They sat down on the faintly green, as though grass-stained, ground in front of the cave. It was very cold in the shade and the sea breeze spanked their faces. Ryuji bundled into his pea coat and crossed his legs. He had just settled himself when the bulldozers began their din again.

"Well, have any of you guys ever been aboard a really big ship?" he ventured, with forced cheeriness.

They glanced around at each other, but no one answered.

"You talk about life at sea," he began again, facing his stolid audience, "you have to begin with getting seasick. Any sailor's been through it one time or another. And I've known men to throw in the towel after one cruise, they've had such a hell of a time with it. The larger the ship is, the more mixing of rolling and pitching you get; and there are some special smells too, like paint and oil and food cooking in the galley. . . ."

When he saw they weren't interested in seasickness, he tried a song for lack of anything else. "Did you fellas ever hear this song?

"The whistle wails and streamers tear,
    Our ship slips away from the pier.
Now the sea's my home, I decided that.
But even I must shed a tear
    As I wave, boys, as I wave so sad.
    At the harbor town where my heart was glad."

The boys nudged each other and giggled, and finally burst out laughing. Noboru was embarrassed to death. He stood up abruptly and, plucking Ryuji's cap from his head, turned his back on the others and began to toy with it.

The anchor at the center of the large, tear-shaped

emblem was girded with chains of gold thread and wreathed in laurel branches embroidered in gold and hung with silver berries. Above and below the emblem, hawsers of gold braid were looped in slack coils. The peak was bleak: reflecting the afternoon sun, it shone with a mournful luster.

Once, at sunset on a summer day, this marvelous cap had receded over a dazzling sea, becoming a glittering emblem of farewell and the unknown. This very cap, receding until it was free of the high injunctions of existence, had become an exalted firebrand lighting the way to eternity!

"My first voyage was on a freighter bound for Hong Kong. . . ." As he began to talk about his career, Ryuji felt the boys growing more attentive. He told them of his experiences on that first voyage, the failures, the confusion, the longing, and the melancholy. Then he started on anecdotes collected on voyages around the world: waiting in Suez harbor for clearance through the canal when someone discovered that one of the hawsers had been stolen; the watchman in Alexandria who spoke Japanese and conspired with merchants on the pier to foist various vulgar items on the crew (details of these Ryuji withheld as being unsuitable material for the classroom); the unimaginable difficulty of taking on coal at Newcastle in Australia and then readying the ship for the next load before they reached Sydney, a journey logged in a single watch; encoun-

tering off the coast of South America a United Fruit
transport vessel and the sea air suddenly redolent of the
tropical fruit brimming in the hatches. . . .

Halfway through his story, Ryuji happened to glance
up and saw the leader slipping on a pair of long latex
gloves. Tensing his fingers, the boy crossed them nervously again and again as if to glue the cold rubber to
his flesh.

Ryuji ignored him. A bright student bored with
class was acting on a caprice—a meaningless display.
Besides, the more he talked, the more insistently recol-
lection was prodding him; turning, he gazed at the thin
line of condensed blue which was the sea.

Trailing black smoke, a small ship was teetering on
the horizon. He could have been aboard that ship himself. Gradually, as he talked to the boys, Ryuji had
come to understand himself as Noboru imagined him.

I could have been a man sailing away forever. He
had been fed up with all of it, glutted, and yet now,
slowly, he was awakening again to the immensity of
what he had abandoned.

The dark passions of the tides, the shriek of a tidal
wave, the avalanching break of surf upon a shoal . . . an
unknown glory calling for him endlessly from the dark
offing, glory merged in death and in a woman, glory to
fashion of his destiny something special, something
rare. At twenty he had been passionately certain: in the
depths of the world's darkness was a point of light

which had been provided for him alone and would draw near someday to irradiate him and no other.

Whenever he dreamed of them, glory and death and woman were consubstantial. Yet when the woman had been attained, the other two withdrew beyond the offing and ceased their mournful wailing of his name. The things he had rejected were now rejecting him.

Not that the blast furnace of a world had ever been his to call his own, but once he had felt the sun fasten on his flank beneath the tropical palms he missed so much and gnaw his flesh with sharp, hot teeth. Now only embers remained. Now began a peaceful life, a life bereft of motion.

Now perilous death had rejected him. And glory, no doubt of that. And the retching drunkenness of his own feelings. The piercing grief, the radiant farewells. The call of the Grand Cause, another name for the tropical sun; and the women's gallant tears, and the dark longing, and the sweet heavy power propelling him toward the pinnacle of manliness—now all of this was done, finished.

"Want some tea?" The leader's high, clear voice rang out behind him.

"Okay. . . ." Ryuji mused on without even turning his head. He recalled the shapes of islands he had visited. Makatea in the South Pacific and New Caledonia. The West Indies: seething with languor and melancholy, teeming with condor and parrots and, everywhere you looked, palms. Emperor palms. Wine palms. Surging out of the splendor of the sea, death had swept down on him like a stormy bank of clouds. A vision of death now eternally beyond his reach, majestic, acclaimed, heroic death unfurled its rapture across his brain. And if the world had been provided for just this radiant death, then why shouldn't the world also perish for it!

Waves, as tepid as blood, inside an atoll. The tropical sun blaring across the sky like the call of a brass trumpet. The many-colored sea. Sharks. . . .

Another step or two and Ryuji would have regretted it.

"Here's your tea," Noboru offered from behind him, thrusting a dark-brown plastic cup near Ryuji's cheek. Absently, Ryuji took it. He noticed Noboru's hand trembling slightly, probably from the cold.

Still immersed in his dream, he drank down the tepid tea. It tasted bitter. Glory, as anyone knows, is bitter stuff.

Library of Japanese Literature

FOLK LEGENDS OF JAPAN by *Richard M. Dorson*

FOOTPRINTS IN THE SNOW by *Kenjiro Tokutomi; translated by Kenneth Strong*

FORBIDDEN COLORS by *Yukio Mishima; translated by Alfred H. Marks*

FRIENDS by *Kobo Abé; translated by Donald Keene*

GEISHA IN RIVALRY by *Kafū Nagai; translated by Kurt Meissner, with the collaboration of Ralph Friedrich*

GLEANINGS IN BUDDHA-FIELDS: Studies of Hand and Soul in the Far East by *Lafcadio Hearn*

THE GOSSAMER YEARS: The Diary of a Noble-woman of Heian Japan *translated by Edward Seiden-sticker*

GRASS ON THE WAYSIDE by *Sōseki Natsume; translated by Edwin McClellan*

HARP OF BURMA by *Michio Takeyama; translated by Howard Hibbett*

THE HEIKE STORY by *Eiji Yoshikawa; translated by Uenaka Uramatsu*

A HISTORY OF JAPANESE LITERATURE by *William George Aston*

HOMECOMING by *Jirō Osaragi; translated by Brewster Horwitz, with an introduction by Harold Strauss*

THE HUNTING GUN by *Yasushi Inoue; translated by Sadamichi Yokoö and Sanford Goldstein*

I AM A CAT by *Sōseki Natsume; translated by Aiko Ito and Graeme Wilson*

IN GHOSTLY JAPAN by *Lafcadio Hearn*

MADAME DE SADE *by Yukio Mishima; translated by Donald Keene*

THE MAKIOKA SISTERS *by Junichirō Tanizaki; translated by Edward G. Seidensticker*

MODERN JAPANESE LITERATURE: From 1868 to Present Day *compiled and edited by Donald Keene*

MODERN JAPANESE STORIES: An Anthology *edited by Ivan Morris, with translations by Edward Seidensticker, George Saito, Geoffrey Sargent, and Ivan Morris*

NIHONGI: Chronicles of Japan from the Earliest Times to A.D. 697 *translated from the original Chinese and Japanese by William George Aston*

OUT OF THE EAST: Reveries and Studies in New Japan *by Lafcadio Hearn*

A PERSONAL MATTER *by Kenzaburō Oë; translated by John Nathan*

THE PORNOGRAPHERS *by Akiyuki Nozaka; translated by Michael Gallagher*

RASHOMON AND OTHER STORIES *by Ryūnosuke Akutagawa; translated by Takashi Kojima*

THE ROMANCE OF THE MILKY WAY AND OTHER STUDIES AND STORIES *by Lafcadio Hearn*

THE RUINED MAP *by Kobo Abé; translated by E. Dale Saunders*

CHARLES E. TUTTLE CO.: PUBLISHERS
Suido 1-chome, 2-6, Bunkyo-ku, Tokyo, Japan